DEDICATION

I dedicate this book to all the great thinkers and artists, of all genders and sexual identities, who made the Renaissance possible.

I would further like to dedicate this to all the people who have been marginalized or persecuted for being different, all throughout history.

ACKNOWLEDGMENTS

I would like to thank all those who helped me along the way with this book, especially Heather, Cindy, Bob, Stephanie, Sharon, David, Marcus, Paulino, and my husband, Antonio, without whose love and support this project would not have been possible.

"Time stays long enough for anyone who will use it."
–Leonardo da Vinci

This is a translation of something found, along with a right-to-left version, presumably copied by Leonardo da Vinci's assistant, Franceso Melzi, between the pages of an old book in a library in Tours, France.

Amboise, France, 1518

Dear Cecho,

I have waited too long to write these memoirs; as such, I think it would be easier if I consider this a kind of letter to you, *amore mio*, at least for now.

Though you know and love your Leo well, and have for years, there are secrets of my heart, as well as depths of my mind, that you still do not grasp. I presume to think you would like to plumb these, especially since you have been urging me for years to write such a thing.

Where to start?

Who is, after all, Leonardo of Vinci? Or rather, who *was* he?

LEONARDO'S LETTER

I was one of the greatest minds of my age, despite so many flaws. I brought forth works that make me almost burst with pride just to think of them. I once diverted a river. I served dukes, kings, and popes. I soared to great heights, only to come crashing down like a crippled wren. I am physically ruined, can barely walk, and my right arm scarcely moves. Where once pulsed youthful beauty and charm, now I see only decay, and my once-lovely face has been ravaged by the cruelty of time. I am haunted by the constant nightmare of destructive floods. I am racked both by torturous pain and the wrenching sadness that comes from haunting a body that no longer really works. I was pursued by a lifelong enemy who nearly defeated me. I fear that life has lost all meaning, and that mine, especially, has had precious little. I am living in exile.

And yet…and yet, my mind remains surprisingly sharp. My left arm, the important one, still does obey me, and I have things to say and do before I go. I can walk a bit. I am, somehow and against all odds, still here. And, miracle of miracles, I have *you*, my dear Cecho, at my side, both day and night. And your love is, lest I forget, a joy I experience every one of my living days.

One thing I wish to make clear, to anyone who may one day peruse these pages, is that writing the story of my life was *not* my idea.

It was, rather, that of Francesco, my devoted disciple and dearest friend, for whom I am writing this. He is the best love an eccentric old man such as I could ever desire.

And now that my great enemy is gone—or so I believe—I deem it safe finally to put quill to paper and record these thoughts.

My enemy.

He tried to destroy me, to crush the great Leonardo. But I was not to be broken, and I am not to be trifled with, even in this sorry state, so late in the autumn of my life. When have you ever known me to surrender, much less admit defeat? No. Not then, not now. Not ever!

Despite the rumors, there has been only one man I truly hated, whose name I refuse to use. More on him later.

For now, let me dispel a rumor, that of my supposed hatred of Michelangelo Buonarroti. To be frank: Michelangelo was merely a pest, an amateur rival barely worthy of mention. I am a man of great love and expansive, almost universal kindness. It takes a special kind of evil to make *me* hate someone. Despite everything, that foolish sculptor generated no such animus. Part of me almost feels *sorry* for him, and wishes him success in the Vatican, where he currently resides, or so I hear.

Of course, on the other hand, there have also been only two men I have ever truly *loved*, both, coincidentally, named Francesco. One was a kind bachelor uncle who showed me great affection and taught me all he could about the world. The other is *you*, my dearest one. You have made my later years more wonderful than I could ever have imagined.

LEONARDO'S LETTER

It must be said, however, to any future reader — that is, if Cecho allows this ever to be seen by anyone: I will probably abandon this project. Why deny it? I am old now, and I am fully aware of my own faults. I am not only an incorrigible procrastinator, but I often fail to follow through with projects that I *do* start and love.

Francesco, my *Cecho*, you have often said that a record of my life deserves to be left for posterity. But what do I care for such things? I often seem incapable of success even when I *intend* to create something!

I endeavored once to bring forth my *magnum opus*, a great painting in Milan that would inspire everyone through the fire of my faith and the height of my talent; alas, it is but a dismal failure that will soon slip into mere oblivion. *Sic transit gloria mundi.*

Most of what I have attempted has been a pathetic disappointment, at least to me. I accept my fate. Instead of changing the world, I would now be content just to leave its stage with a tiny shred of dignity intact.

I am *not* one of those pathetic prattlers who write reams of nonsense and inflict their endless expertise and tiresome reflections on anyone who will read or listen. I have grown rebellious and uncooperative, like a boy of thirteen. Francesco accuses me of being an unrepentant curmudgeon ever since our move to this northern place, where the sun's warmth is a far cry from Tuscany's, and where I pass my final days wandering the banks of the Loire as a guest of the King of France. The peasants here must think I am a curious sight as I shuffle by!

I often wonder if everyone here thinks I waste my time, as well as that of the king. I catch people whispering about how I spend my final days as a fool, stubbornly refusing to put my genius and talents to good use.

When Francesco implies such things, I gently remind him that I still fill the pages of my notebooks with all manner of calculations, sketches, and reflections, and continue to work on my unfinished masterpiece, the one I carry with me everywhere, the lovely Lisa who stares at me every day propped up against an old brown trunk, a gentle smile tugging at her lips.

What I mean to say is that I still have things to do and much to learn. *Ancora imparo,* as some old men in Florence like to say, and it is true, because I *am* still learning new things. Learning never exhausts the mind, after all. Part of me suspects that I could drop dead tomorrow, and then another part wonders if, as my great enemy was somehow able to do, I could persist even further into an absurd old age.

Of course, as much as I prattle on about my bitterness and bad temper, I suppose I fool no one. My great enemy was one who seemed powered by a stubborn, cynical, despicable hatred and, yes, I will say it: evil. In short, he was too mean to die. I am not such a man. I imagine that I will pass with a beatific smile on my lips.

LEONARDO'S LETTER

Life well spent is long. And mine has been both.

As I often say, I love those who can smile in trouble, who can gather strength from distress, and grow brave by reflection. I have smiled and laughed much in my mad life, and I have grown stronger because of the many challenges.

I hope that this time of reflection will help me grow braver as I prepare to meet my maker, the thought of which, if I am being honest, scares me, if you will pardon the pun, half to death.

Well, then, you may very well ask, what of the task at hand? What of Leonardo's Letter to his beloved Cecho?

Alas...what everyone eventually learns about me, and that, you, Cecho, know best of all, is that, when I do or learn something new, usually through trial and error (*"experientia docet"* is my motto), I do it for *myself* and to satisfy my *own* pantheist love of variety. This is, of course, why I left a checkered pattern of incomplete projects in my wake over the decades. I have a thirst for knowledge, a love of learning that far exceeds any other ambition. That is why, even at this advanced age, Cecho, you usually need to coax me to bed after an evening of reading and writing. I am simply too interested in my numerous projects to be bogged down by any *one* project, and I have always been that way.

I have often thought that people should be *impressed* with how little I have changed, instead of acting frustrated by my wondrous consistency. It is not as if my character should be any great surprise by now.

That is enough for one night. Perhaps I will write a bit more tomorrow.

LEONARDO'S LETTER

The Garden of Vinci

As a personal favor to you, Cecho, *amore mio*, and for that reason only, I will continue this silly task, at least for now.

Shall I tell of my early years in and around Vinci? Should I wax poetic about the dew on the grass of the orchards surrounding my grandfather's home, and the apple tree up which I would climb? How innocent and free my childhood was! I could write page after page about how I used to run naked through the fields and swim in the stream at the bottom of a ravine, how I nearly broke my neck as I slipped on a rock while trying to catch mayflies as a boy.

It is true, I used to climb the hills and mountains around Vinci and Anchiano as a child, which kept me from my studies. My father hired an ancient monk to tutor me, but the old fool gave up trying to force knowledge into me after a while. Once he told me about the Great Flood, the one that had destroyed the world; I refused to learn anything more from him. I was haunted by frightful dreams after that, and I would hide when I saw him coming, sometimes in a closet in Uncle Francesco's alcove.

Francesco was fifteen years my senior, and he often felt more like an older brother than an uncle. He sometimes seemed to me the man my father *could* have been, had my parent known laughter and been blessed with a tender heart. My uncle, on the other hand, always showed me kindness, and encouraged my adventurous nature.

The world was mine to explore, and my uncle, my favorite teacher.

He used to sit with me in the green meadows and the two of us would examine lizards, plants, and insects together. Once, we even dissected a dead frog to see how it looked on the inside. He helped me collect moths and butterflies, and we studied their cut-apart bodies, once they were pinned to a small wooden board that he gave me for my saint's day.

He told me that all of nature was God's expression of love toward man, His greatest creation. He said that, since the hills were clad in the most beautiful wildflowers, these were the finest clothes in the whole wide world.

An important thing to know about me as a boy is that I had a fascination for swirls, twirls, and spirals of all kinds. I can remember the first time I peered into a small pool beside a stream, and took notice of my own capricious curls, and of their mysterious golden hue.

Cecho, you will no doubt think me a vain and vile narcissist, but we had no mirror at home, and I was enchanted not only by my own reflection, but also by the curious curves and lovely lines framing my face. What caused my blond locks to be so curly, while those of my mother were straight and honey-brown? Soon, I found myself studying the eddies in the nearby stream, fascinated by the way the energy of the water bounced and played off the stones and rocks, and how the patterns seemed ever-changing. I wanted to understand the mysteries of this world, both large and small.

Luckily, since very little was expected of me, nature was, in a way, my childhood classroom.

I often thank God I had the good luck to be born a bastard, and thus denied the tedium of following in my father's footsteps as a notary. Although we never spoke of it, I suspect that Father was relieved to pass me off to my master, Verrocchio, as soon as my voice began to change, instead of going to the trouble of legitimating the whelp he had produced with a lowly peasant girl. But now, I suppose I am getting ahead of myself.

(Cecho urges me to create a chronological narrative, but he, above all others, knows that this is not my way. I think that, perhaps, I will instead simply write thematically, jumping from one topic to another, and hope that Cecho, or another reader, can keep up, or piece together a more linear narrative of my life, if that is what he chooses.)

For the record, let me say that I find this entire exercise silly as, not only do I waste *my* time with this, but I hate the idea of you wasting your time, Cecho, recopying my left-handed scrawl in a way that others can read it. "What others?" I never tire of asking. In twenty years, no one will even remember who Leonardo of Vinci was. But then, you say, I should stop indulging in false modesty, claiming that I know very *well* how much I may be remembered. I am not being false, however; I have no doubts about my *own* worth, but I *do* doubt how little my fellow men value such things, excepting, perhaps, the fortunate few owners of works I was able to complete, and a small coterie of friends and lovers.

Lovers. Oh, yes, *that* ticklish subject. Not that I care for my reputation, mind you; the rumors have followed me like a stench since that first accusation when I was barely more than a youth in Florence in the year of grace 1476. Luckily, my enemy, the one who almost got me killed, is finally, almost certainly, no longer a threat. But more on him later.

Even though I never pretended to be that which I am not, is it wrong of me to urge you, my dear Francesco, to bury these scribblings? Perhaps you could hide them in a library, slipping them between the raspy pages of some forgotten, dusty folio. At least for a while, that is. I suppose that, if one were to find this manuscript someday, hopefully long after I am gone, whatever is left of my essence or soul shall regard with amusement the scandalized faces of any eventual readers. In any case, you have urged me to be candid about the details of my life, promising to handle this tale with the utmost discretion for a time if I so desire. If this even turns *into* anything, that is.

Perhaps I will persist. I must confess that the idea of recounting my storied life, like my youthful peering into the "monster cave" of the Tuscan countryside, fills me with fear and, if truth be told, a small bit of joy, a tickle of delicious excitement. It is, as the French call it, *un petit frisson*.

And, so, my dear *Cechino*, it appears that you will get your wish. I will, indeed, pour my heart into these frivolous pages, at least for now, unless, as you and I both suspect may happen, I lose interest and follow a different passion altogether, or if my health takes a turn for the worse. After all, it is clear to anyone watching that my body is shutting down. How much longer can I possibly have?

L'Inizio, the Beginning

Having agreed to embark on this quest, the question is, where to begin?

I will start with the truth of my origins; after all, simplicity is the ultimate sophistication.

I doubt my early years would interest anyone. I am the product of an ill-advised union between my father, a notary from a prominent family, and a country girl named Caterina, with whom he had a tryst in the summer of 1451 while visiting my grandfather, who was living the life of a country squire in the provincial town of Vinci.

As it happens, my *nonno* enjoyed various projects and fancied himself a "gentleman farmer" who had failed to join the family business, that of being a notary. In fact, he was descended from a string of such men stretching back generations. He had married the daughter of a notary and raised my father to be one, even though I cannot ever remember my grandfather practicing that trade himself. In fact, my father's father did not do much of *anything* except grumble and grouse while living off the rents from laborers who produced wine, olive oil, and wheat.

My father, however, was a man who yearned to toil behind a desk. Serious and conservative, he was also more ambitious and diligent than his father. He *had* answered the call and followed in his ancestors' footsteps. Of course, while spending some weeks at home looking after one of Grandfather's orchards, he experienced a momentary lapse in judgment when he spied my lovely mother on her way home from the market. Apparently, they met under a grape arbor, as this place was often pointed out to me as the spot to which I owed my existence, or so went the story when I was young.

I wish I could boast of a better beginning, but there you have it: I seem to have been conceived under a wall of grapes destined to make barely drinkable wine.

Once it became obvious that my mother was with child, Father fled to his comfortable life back in Florence. Luckily for me, my grandfather was, for once, more responsible than Ser Pietro, my progenitor, and he saw to it that my mother was set up in a humble, yet adequate, home in the hamlet of Anchiano, not far from Vinci. My father's family provided Caterina with a warm bed and fireplace, some fresh mutton to nibble on, and even some goat's milk and honey to help her garner strength. When the spring arrived, a midwife was on hand for when I came mewling into the world in April of 1452.

Caterina Lippi was an exceedingly comely young woman. I inherited my good looks from her, not my boring father. And so it was that, though encumbered with a boy born out of wedlock, a *figlio naturale,* or "natural son," as the villagers said euphemistically, it was not long before she caught the eye of a handsome local laborer. My stepfather,

Antonio, whom everyone called *Accatabriga,* married her without delay. She soon had a new family with him, a strapping, strong man, a good man. He got into too many fights, but always provided for Caterina and her children. He was a farmer and kiln worker. I have very few memories of him, as I was there only a short time.

They say a mother can always tell when her son is a sensitive and special sort, unlikely to marry, and mine was no exception. We had an exceedingly close bond. Even though I left her side quite young, I shall always treasure those first years in her home. For a while, she even entertained the idea of sending me off to be educated as a man of the Church. I bounced back and forth between my mother's home, a modest gray-stone cottage in Anchiano, and my family's property in Vinci.

After I became famous in the world of the arts, all manner of whispers swirled around my mother's identity. I must confess, I never denied them. The idea of her being a Jew, a Moor, one of the gypsies known as *Zincara Roma,* or even a slave from the recently sacked Constantinople gave me, by extension, an air of the exotic. But the truth is, alas, less exciting. My mother was an orphan, a simple country girl, a peasant with a dark complexion, and a sometime wet nurse for hire.

In fact, I was the milk-brother of a man who would later become a lord of the manor near the town of Vinci. To spare her feelings, I never asked if she had seduced my father to have me, and thus obtained that position thanks to breasts replete with milk, but that is what I suspect happened, and the wagging tongues of Anchiano agreed.

Some would be angry to think that such a thing had led to their birth, but not I! I am, and always have been, simply glad to be alive in this world in the first place; what care I for how or why I came to be? Perhaps God put me here for a reason.

In short, Caterina was a beauty, and knew how to get what she wanted. I inherited this skill from her, and attribute my playful, pagan, and sensual nature to her completely. I also believe that the lovely curls and honey-colored eyes of my youth came from my mother's side. It is for some reason, my dear Cecho, that so many wanted me to model for them in the workshops and *bodegas* of Florence. My image and physique shall live on for centuries, after all, in colorful paintings and rippling marble.

In any case, back to my parents. Obviously, a marriage between my father and mother was out of the question. However, I will give my *paterfamilias* his due, as he eventually did what he could for us. He helped my grandfather and uncle with expenses related to my upkeep and rudimentary education. And, when the time was right, he took me to Florence from the untamed Vinci countryside.

What more can I tell you about myself, and my character when I was a boy?

When she lived with me in later years, Caterina told me stories, such as how I used to pester her always with questions, as I was a curious and precocious child. I was also a creative and dramatic sort, and I used to put on puppet shows for the neighborhood children. I can still remember her, perched on a stool in the corner of our hovel, an apron between her knees as she shucked peas and beans for our evening soup, laughing in delight at my many voices. I would often entertain her with a simple *commedia dell'arte*. I recall a play about a nobleman whose mistress, a fishmonger's daughter, chased him around the kitchen with a butcher knife. For this, I designed décor and costumes, and improvised a silly script. I suppose it was impressive for a boy of five.

Not long after, I went to live with my paternal family for good. Soon after I was born, my father had wed the sixteen year-old Albiera, who became quite fond of me by the time she was ready to become a mother herself. I think she imagined I would help take care of the children she planned to have with my father, and it is true, I would have done just that, and my life could have taken a vastly different turn had I become a doting "uncle" dedicated to the care of children.

Since she was so young, Albiera felt like an older sister to me, and we got on quite well. Unfortunately, she lost several babies in a row, and I was always the one to comfort and care for her in the aftermath of each such tragedy. I remember singing to her, rocking her like a child, and holding onto her as she trembled in grief.

LEONARDO'S LETTER

My father and grandfather found our grief and distress misplaced over these lost babes; I remember each of them snapping at Albiera to dry her tears, claiming that she could always have more children. They all but came out and said that her only function, indeed, was to carry on the family lineage and never to complain.

This rapport I had with Albiera pushed my father to take more of an interest in me, especially once my uncle told him how special he thought I was. Had it not been for Albiera and my uncle, I imagine my father might have forgotten about me altogether.

On one memorable visit back to Vinci, my father, who normally was away in Florence, witnessed my skill as an artist, and this would have huge repercussions for my future.

Since Uncle Francesco had told him of my many natural talents, Father decided to put them to the test. He made me decorate a shield for a local nobleman. He gave me wood from a fig tree and had me design a fearsome head for it, like that of Medusa. My hope was that the fear inspired by the shield would protect its bearer better than any fighting could. I spent days studying the anatomy of a lizard, which I drew on the wooden panel, and then painted a fearsome picture with elaborate colors of the most gruesome beast imaginable. It appeared to poison the very air with its fiery breath, and its dragon face seemed to emerge from dark, broken rocks, spewing venom from gaping jaws, spitting fire from its eyes and hissing smoke from its nostrils. I still remember, sixty years on, how Father recoiled in horror at the sight, before a subtle smile settled on his lips. He regarded me in silence, and I felt I could read his thoughts: "This boy will surpass me in every way." And, indeed, I have.

I heard that Father gave a poor copy of that shield to the nobleman, but sold *my* shield to the Duke of Milan, where I would follow years later.

"You are too sensitive, and far too smart for your own good, Leonardo," my father reproached me.

At first, I thought he was joking, but then I realized he was serious. "The world doesn't like people who are *too* talented, who make others look bad," he continued. "Men can be jealous and cruel, especially to those who are different," he explained. It would be years before I learned what he meant.

"Also, never forget that you are an illegitimate son, and a left-handed one at that," he said. "People will always suspect you of something sinister, no matter *how* good you are."

"Yes, Father," I said, wondering why he was telling *me* all of this. Was he trying to protect me, or make me feel bad? I thought of how the old friar had warned him that I was no good, a boy in danger of becoming a pawn of the Devil. Was *this* what worried Father? Or was he afraid that I would forget my place?

"You are *non legitimo*," he would repeat, over, and over again, as if it were *my* fault. "The Guild of Judges and Notaries will never let you in, so we'll have to find something *else* for you," he admonished.

It was true. This conservative guild, formed in 1197, to which generations of men in my family had belonged, demanded that its members be of the utmost trustworthiness. Even a bastard who had been legitimated would be a *persona non grata* among them.

"We will have to find something else for you to do," he would say, again and again, *ad nauseam*. "Although, what that may be, I have no idea. You don't act like other boys your age, so I have no notion of what we can find for you, as you *will* have to earn your own wages and support yourself. You won't inherit *anything* from me, assuming I have other children."

"I know, Father," I would say with a sigh.

I could not figure out how my father truly felt about me. I knew I would have to be subordinate to any legitimate children he might have with Albiera, a wife who was the daughter of a prominent businessman. Sometimes he seemed proud of me, but at other times, he seemed keen to get *rid* of me. Perhaps I embarrassed him. However, I wanted to tell him, it was not *my* fault that I had been born out of wedlock. And it is not like I had *chosen* to be different. I just was who I was, a child of God like anyone else. Uncle Francesco had said so.

My beloved uncle instilled not only a love of nature in me, but also an appreciation of poetry, even though I was more gifted in other areas, and not so much in literature. However, years before my tutor forced me to memorize parts of the Bible, including several psalms, my uncle would sit with me in the grass and recite parts of his favorite one, Psalm 147, which he claimed had been composed by King David himself to express how much God loved the world and all of creation. One night, while sitting looking up at the night sky, he exclaimed:

"Praise the Lord. He heals the brokenhearted and binds up their wounds. He determines the number of stars and calls them each by name. He covers the sky with clouds; He supplies the earth with rain and makes the grass grow on the hills. He provides food for the cattle and for the young ravens when they call. His pleasure is not in the strength of the horse, nor his delight in the legs of the warrior; the Lord delights in those who fear Him, who put their hope in His unfailing love."

I pictured King David sitting outside on a night like this, feeling a light drizzle on his face perhaps, and writing this psalm in praise of all that is good in the world. Perhaps he wrote it in the company of his dearest friend and companion, Jonathan, whose very name showed that he was a gift from God for David.

Could I be one of those who put their unfailing hope and love in God? Would He send me a friend I could love as much as David loved Jonathan?

(Cecho, I would say that, finally in my old age, God has done so. He sent me you, after all!)

*

One thing I can say about myself when I was young, as well as now: I have always been a seeker.

One tale I often tell when asked about my early years is of the time I went out exploring around Vinci, at the age of eight or nine, and came to the mouth of a great cave. I was struck by the sure knowledge that frightening mysteries lurked therein. I fancied it a place of monsters and dragons, like the one I had designed for that wooden shield. However, I remember being seized by two delicious and contradictory feelings: that of the fear of the unknown at whose precipice I was perched, and that of the curiosity of what I could discover if I abandoned the safety of the world I knew outside the cave.

Curiosity and fear, two emotions that exist like intertwining serpents for all seekers in this world.

Of course, I embraced my fear and plunged forward into the aperture after running home to fetch a candle with which to illuminate that hitherto undiscovered place. I remember the unforgettable *frisson* that shook my body that day, as I held aloft the candle in that dark space. My childish mind was full of awe as I inspected the scattered collection of strange bones of what I imagined was a long-lost sea leviathan.

A swarm of questions ran through my mind as I puzzled over this find. How came these bones to rest here? Why were they now turned to stone? Had this land once been covered in water? Had it all happened during Noah's Great Flood? Or was there more to the story of Earth and Heaven than what I had been taught in the ancient church of Vinci and at my rustic country school?

Years later, I would correspond with a man named Rodrigo who had sailed with Columbus to a new land across the Ocean Sea. He told of huge, strange creatures of blue, black, and white, sticking their heads out of the water, and even jumping into the air.

Now I wonder if perhaps this beast, whose bones I saw scattered before me, had been one of those monsters?

Once, as I said, my tutor had made me read aloud the story of Noah and the Great Flood. I do not know why, but I became obsessed with the idea of another great flood sweeping down to destroy the world.

What if God turned his fickle wrath toward me, and decided to punish us again, drowning everyone I knew and cared about? This obsession grabbed hold of my fevered imagination. When I thought of the creature I had seen in the cavern, trapped, thrashing about, unable to move as the rising waters locked him into an aquatic grave, a sense of dread came over me and haunted my nightmares.

Another thing troubled me about that day when I had explored the "monster cave." I had found all sorts of small bits of stone that looked like shells in there. How had that cave, which was on the side of a mountain, come to be filled with *shells*? Had that place once been covered by the waters of the sea? How many floods had washed over my beloved Tuscany? Were there *more* than what the Bible mentioned?

I have lived with these mysteries all my life, and the curiosity inspired by questions such as these pushes me always to plunge ahead, even when common sense would lead me in a safer direction.

Despite the worry, how glad I am that I forced myself into that cave! I now realize that everything I have ever done, all that I am, and the man I have become, can be traced to that one moment.

I have always been impressed with the urgency of *doing*. Knowing is not enough; we must apply what we learn. Being *willing* is not enough; we must act, we must *do* things.

Most men lead lives of placid uneventfulness; I am proud to boast of having followed a much different path.

I have realized that people of accomplishment rarely sit back and just let things happen to them. Instead, they went out and happened to *things*, and that was what I decided to do as a young man.

So, you may wonder, why fill so many notebooks, such as this one, with random thoughts and observations? Why the queries and hypotheses, tumbling out one after another? Why the endless lists? To what end the countless notes on themes like the effects of light in paintings, to every aspect of flight, to queries on the tongues of birds?

One word sums it all up: curiosity.

I was overcome, ever since that day in the cave, with an insatiable curiosity. From that moment, I have been driven by an unquenchable thirst. I wanted to know everything. I yearned to see how machines worked, to create a myriad of fantastical inventions. I aimed to study human corpses and learn every vein, muscle, and sinew. This would help me become the greatest artist that ever lived!

I wanted to fly with the birds and then plunge deep into the sea.

I wondered about things that most people stop thinking about as children; I asked why the sky is blue and why dogs bark and why the muscles of a stallion ripple when it runs.

I wanted to know it all.

The noblest pleasure of all is the joy of understanding.

Perhaps I felt I could come to know the very nature of God through my quest.

And here is where my awful hubris came in:

I knew I was smart enough to do it.

LEONARDO'S LETTER

I know that this is quite a claim to make for one with so little formal schooling. It is true, my father only gave me a rudimentary education. Father assumed, as did everyone, that I would never leave Vinci, or if I did, I would become a simple Florentine tradesman working in the shadow of *Il Duomo*, perhaps perfecting the flourishes of some goldsmith on Florence's great bridge, the *Ponte Vecchio*. Few people expected anything from me. Even fewer people, possibly only my uncle Francesco, could have predicted I would teach myself Latin and become a voracious reader, amassing an impressive collection of books ranging from botany and Arabic mathematics to Pliny's histories and even staged comedies of the previous century. I even dabbled a bit in the recent Florentine masters of the written word, such as Boccaccio, Petrarch, and Dante, although these last three were far from my favorites. After reading so much in Latin, it was a relief to read something in our own Tuscan tongue, although even Dante seemed old-fashioned by my time.

Of course, I admit I was skeptical, to say the least, of the methods most men had long used to gain what I call "received knowledge." I believed, instead, that everything we know has its origins in our perceptions.

Our knowledge of Nature begins with reason and ends in experience. As such, it is sometimes necessary for us, as thinkers, trying to glean patterns and meaning, to start with experience and, from this, we must proceed to investigate the reasons for what we perceive.

Since the Roman Empire, my countrymen have had their sons (and sometimes, their daughters) educated first by pedagogic slaves, and then by specialized tutors. Churchmen had truths handed down since time immemorial in the Scholastic Tradition, which, as far as I can tell, took everything Aristotle said, mixed it with Christianity a few centuries ago, and then passed it down for everyone to accept without question.

That was decidedly *not* my style.

Of course, it was my great luck to be born in the time of the Medici, the great patrons of Florence. But I would not realize this for many years to come.

I will say it again: *sono stato molto fortunato*. I was most fortunate to have been born when and where I was. But we all know that luck, as well as talent, can be a curse not unlike the unhappy touch of Midas.

As the old priest of our village used to say, *sic transit gloria mundi*. Any glory that we may touch in this world is merely transitory; as soon as it appears, it slips through our fingers and is gone.

Furthermore, as my father was always quick to point out, even though my family was well-connected, I was what I was, and would face many obstacles in life. I knew not to expect or hope for too much glory in this world.

LEONARDO'S LETTER

In moments of fear or self-doubt, my uncle Francesco was always there to listen and comfort me. One day, he invited me to take a walk with him by the stream.

"I know you're rather...*preoccupied* right now, Leonardo," he said.

To this, I simply nodded.

"You're starting to grow up," he said. "Soon, you will realize just how difficult life can be for those who are different."

I had no idea how to respond, so stood staring into the stream without saying a word.

"I know you're always thinking of the power of water," he said, after a long moment. "I know you're afraid of a great flood coming one day to wash us all away, and that you're obsessed with the many turns and swirls of it all."

I smiled a bit despite myself. My uncle was so perceptive, picking up on things unsaid. I always wondered how he knew what he knew.

"Look at that big rock in the stream there," he told me. "Notice how the water flows happily along, and all of a sudden it comes into contact with something that seems strong, blocking its path."

I nodded, wondering where he was going with all of this.

"*You* are like the water, Leonardo," he said, a smile illuminating his face. "When you come up against formidable barriers, as you will, you will just have to find a way *around* them," he said. "This is because, dear *nipote*, you are strong and supple, you are clever and quick. You can adapt. You are simply *better* than any obstacle you will come up against," he said. "Just learn to go around, then find your own way."

And find my own way I have.

Alas, I would enjoy writing page after page about my uncle, but for now, on with the story.

The year was 1464. My father had returned to the country estate, and I was a pupil in a humble country school. My grandfather had recently died, which was sad, but this brought me and my uncle even closer together. Uncle Francesco read to me and taught me everything he could, while encouraging every one of my fancies. I was well-liked by the people of Vinci, and Albiera loved me. I thought I was about to become a big brother, as my young stepmother had finally been able to make it to the end of a pregnancy. I was happy and excited. Everything seemed perfect.

Then, when I was almost thirteen, tragedy struck.

Albiera died in childbirth.

Alas, I was never able to mourn her, as I had to take care of my father, who was plunged into a sadness so deep that he needed to flee our idyllic home in Vinci. I believe that he was the kind of man who cannot bear to be alone, needing to occupy himself with various pursuits to help him forget his young wife, whom he had truly loved.

Therefore, he asked me to go with him to Florence.

I could have remained behind in that bucolic paradise of childhood; it was a happy and easy place in which to live. I could have become a farmer, a merchant, or perhaps a teacher at the abacus school. But something told me that *this* was my chance for something more. I could not remain in that place after having plunged into the "monster cave" and lived to tell about it.

I packed a bag and set off with Father on foot, imagining that I could return home if I wanted to.

I could not know it then, but my father had a specific reason for keeping me away from his brother, my uncle Francesco. It was something I would learn many years later. He feared something in our nature.

However, unfortunately for my father, a tiger cannot change his stripes.

We took a carriage to a place overlooking my new home. I remember that we stopped the conveyance and got out, standing on a belvedere on the old Roman road overlooking the city. We gazed upon the thick walls that ran parallel to the Arno.

Father asked me to look down at the Tuscan capital as it stretched out before us. A line of Cyprus trees and myrtle had blocked much of the view, but now Florence lay there in all her golden splendor.

"You can still go back, Leonardo," my father said. "But *I* shall not return to Vinci. Too many memories." He turned to face me. I noticed his thick red velvet doublet and hose, the brown and green feather as it danced in his vermillion cap, and I wondered if I would ever dress that way.

"You can still go back," he repeated, looking down again as he ran his hands over a short brown beard. The sadness in his eyes was replaced by a momentary twinkle, and he raised his eyes to meet mine. "But…I think a great future lies in store for *both* of us if you accompany me." We spent a long moment gazing down again at the city below.

"Just look at that marvelous place. You are *so* gifted, my son." My father turned once again to face me. "I've shown your drawings to a friend, and he thinks you have a great talent. It won't be easy, but you have a chance to really *be* someone in Florence." He paused, as if to let this point sink in. "I won't let you go home again once you come with me through that gate," he added.

"Your room is being turned into a maid's quarters even as we speak. It's now or never, Leonardo. This is your chance."

I briefly hesitated, but then I nodded, hoping I had made the right choice.

LEONARDO'S LETTER

    My father and I walked down that hill and through Florence's Porta San Miniato. I felt giddy with the excitement that came from knowing that I was embracing my destiny. And yet, this was mixed with the sadness of knowing that I was leaving my childhood behind, and there was no going back.

Firenze, Florence

My father, Ser Piero, allowed himself an appropriate mourning period before seeking out the second of his four wives. In the meantime, he threw himself like a drowning man into his work as a notary. In this capacity, he represented, among others, various religious orders, monasteries, the Florentine Jewish community, and, luckily for me, the powerful Medici family. I was fortunate, as his connections often helped me find work when the time came. He worked in the *Palazzo del Podestà*, near the main seat of power in Florence, and I rarely saw him. Father had a small *palazzo* of his own not far from where he worked, but I never felt like more than just a visitor there.

I spent exactly one day with my parent at his notary desk. That was all it took for me to realize that, even if I *had* wanted him to legitimate me and try, against all odds, to find me a place in the guild, that was no life for me. I could think of nothing duller than spending my days drawing up contracts for land sales, wills, and other such things in Latin, which I did not read or write well at the time. Father noted my restlessness, and any doubt he had concerning my ability to do this kind of work vanished faster than he could wave his pen.

Of course, we both knew what destiny had in store for me, but it was important to be sure that following in his footsteps was *not* the path for young Leonardo.

Uncle Francesco had once said that if I followed my destiny, it would save me, but if I denied my true path, it would destroy me.

Within days of our arrival, Father brought me to meet Andrea Del Verrocchio, to whom he had shown my drawings. He agreed to take me on as an apprentice.

Soon, my childhood was over, and I was working from sunup to sundown in Verrocchio's Verrocchio studio.

I always lamented not having more time in my idyllic country home of Vinci. However, the truth must be told: there was no better place in the whole wide world for me than my beloved Florence. I will be so bold as to say that the entire city had been created just for me to explore and flourish in, or at least that is how I felt then, and still do in my vainest moments, which are many.

No longer was Florence a city whose economy depended on simple wool-spinners and agriculture, as had been the case for centuries. Now, an integration of commerce, art, and inventions of all kinds had created a dynamic atmosphere, as well as a growing middle-class. This created a strong market for things of beauty. The city, by the time I got there, was full of merchants, businessmen, architects, goldsmiths, jewelry makers, silk workers, master painters, and artisans of every stripe. I could have continued my formal schooling, but my father saw to it that I got to work right away so that I could be a part of this new reality.

I learned my craft by doing, watching, and listening at the hand of my great master, Verrocchio. He felt that we grow best by performing the work of artists, while living and working alongside them. This included everything from preparing and mixing paints to drawing and hanging cartoons for frescos, while other men talked about the ideas and topics expressed in our work. These themes of the ancients had long lain dormant, and yet were revived in recent years, brought forth and given new life by men such as us. Knowing this made me feel grand, like I was part of something important for the first time in my life. I was an acolyte, initiated into a new priesthood, a brotherhood of men, those dedicated to what we called "the new learning."

One day, while helping Verrocchio paint an angel for a version of *The Baptism of Christ*, Master Andrea paid me a great compliment, though I did not know it at the time.

"Why, you could be the next Giotto," he said with a delighted laugh.

"Who's *that*?" I asked.

A look of shock came over my master's face as my ignorance seemed to scandalize him. I imagine that he wondered at that moment if taking on this provincial, if talented, country lad was worth the trouble.

LEONARDO'S LETTER

"Giotto!" he cried. "He was the most famous artist of the last century, and it's a crime that you don't know of him," he admonished. "Not only was he a painter, a sculptor, an architect, and a poet, but he was a success in Rome with the Pope and died happy and rich," he said. "You, my gifted pupil, have the talent to be like him, the grandfather of Florentine art — *if*," he continued, "you apply yourself, and *if* you can learn not to let your mind wander, and *if* you can somehow get a traditional education."

A traditional education? That was the *last* thing I wanted.

I scoffed at the formal learning of rich young men who filled the piazzas of our Tuscan capital. They had absorbed antiquated ideas from so many dusty old books that had been passed down from generation to generation. They were the pompous fools who, I thought, would dismiss me for a lack of book learning. Well, *I* was a breed apart! I was, after all, a disciple of *experience*!

Day after day, I sat sketching and studying them, an unnoticed presence. I was clad only in my humble artist's smock and short, brown breeches, which rendered me practically invisible in their world. These young men, many of whom were quite handsome, sat dressed as peacocks in rich brocaded doublets, the best hose of all colors, and velvet hats from which plumes sprouted, much like the birds I had studied in the countryside.

The books they discussed had been copied out at great expense onto vellum by underpaid scribes and monks in high towers, or so I imagined. How boring, I thought, how dry and dull, to learn that way, to accept what others wanted to feed us, as if we were babes eating drops from a spoon. This was a new age! Tomorrow belonged to *us*, not them.

I fancied myself a prince of my own kingdom, free to follow my own path. I scoffed at tradition. I only wanted to experiment, and took the time to marvel, to ponder, and to observe nature and the world around me. I cared so little for the written word back then.

Verrocchio must truly have seen my potential, as he gave me all the freedom I craved, provided I helped around the workshop. In time, he seemed to relent in his desire for me to learn the traditional way, and instead let me explore and learn however I saw fit.

I performed experiment after experiment, sometimes making spinning wheels in nearby streams, other times building primitive conveyances drawn by horses, much to the amusement of my new friends. Everything I did was to glean what I could from direct observation. I tried things out in a practical way, seeing if I could cause, and then replicate, what I thought would happen.

However, sometimes Verrocchio would seem to change his mind and insist that I study books or observe others. It was very annoying for one such as I, who could barely pay attention for more than a few minutes at a time.

I began my study of human anatomy around then, as my master wanted me to understand every detail about this subject before allowing me to paint. He demanded that I study the inner workings of the human body, for which he gave me many texts.

I grew to be close friends with a young man who had been apprenticed to a goldsmith before coming to Verrocchio. His name was Alessandro, or Sandro for short, but everyone called him Botticelli, after the man to whom he had previously been apprenticed. I noticed that *he* had the freedom to create as he wished.

"Why doesn't Sandro have to study anatomy before he paints people?" I whined one day. Of course, I should have spared a thought for the fact that my friend was older than I, and he had been in Verrocchio's Verrocchio workshop for years before my father took me there.

"Stop complaining," my master reprimanded. "Sandro doesn't *need* to study the body in order to be a great artist," he said, pausing to draw a line on a cartoon of the *Virgin* and the *Annunciation*. "He already knows how to create bright, beautiful curves and colors that delight the viewer and catch the essence of the human form, especially that of women," he continued. "You, however, Leonardo, need to study how the human body works, what it is made of, bones, veins, organs, all of it. Only *then* can you hope to achieve excellence."

I chafed at these demands, but forced myself to study and learn, usually alone. I knew my mind, and the gaps in my education, better than anyone. Who better to teach me than myself? The last thing I wanted to do was to sit down and be taught in a traditional way, or, worse yet, be forced to read.

However, at some point — dear *Cechino*, please don't ask me to pinpoint when — I shifted my thoughts on this.

It did not come all at once, of course.

As I am sure you are aware, Gutenberg's marvelous printing invention crossed the Alps around the time I came to live in Florence. As if overnight, new techniques for making paper and various improvements to movable type sprung up. Texts could finally be produced *en masse*. Books were no longer just the property of the wealthy; soon, people of the literate middle classes of my dear Florence were buying bound copies at an astonishing rate. I estimate that about one Florentine in three could read in those days, which was likely higher than anywhere else in Europe.

Much to my chagrin, reading was becoming more and more fashionable in my city.

Still, I held off; I thought that books might be nothing but a passing fancy. I still wanted to be the man who learned things for himself, a disciple of experience. "*Experientia docet*" was ever the motto to which I clung, and it still largely is, because experience teaches us better than anything else can.

LEONARDO'S LETTER

Yet I must admit that slowly, despite my best efforts, I found myself seduced by the power of the written word. When I read a German treatise on music with my newly acquired but lackluster Latin, I must admit that I was impressed. Soon, I found myself adjusting both my mellifluous voice and my handheld silver lyre to create ever more beautiful sounds based on what I had read.

For a while, I read little but asked experts in various fields to lecture me on the finer points of whatever they excelled at. But soon, I had to end this practice, as they would turn away or duck into an alleyway if they saw me coming. One man even lied to me, claiming to be the twin of someone I had pestered overly much, and so I realized that I needed to relent, as I was making a nuisance of myself and acquiring the reputation of being something of a bore.

Perish the thought, Cechino; you of all people know how I pride myself at being always in demand, thanks to my pleasant company and congenial nature. Even now, the *last* thing I would ever hope to be is someone whose company is to be avoided. Besides, this expertise in the art of conversation has greatly endeared me to our French hosts.

And, so it was, my dear one, that I was forced to give in to the new technology and adapt to a rapidly changing world, if for no other reason than to salvage my bruised reputation.

Embracing book learning was not a horrible thing, in the end; in fact, I was able to teach myself all sorts of novel subjects and expand my world in marvelous new ways.

How funny that so much knowledge is just waiting there for anyone brave enough to open a book!

It is true; years later, when I went to live at the court of Milan under the protection of Ludovico, *Il Moro,* I often took advantage of his private library. Milan is where I became, dare I say it, an unapologetic bibliophile. Simply put, I read everything I could get my hands on. Of course, this did not stop me from sitting beside the moat of Ludovico's castle in the afternoon studying the wings of birds, as well as those of dragonflies. Nor did it prevent me from bribing men working in morgues of various cities to let me dissect both women and men to help me find out exactly how the human body worked in as much detail as possible. More on all of that later.

Still, I have always believed, and still do so to this day, that we must only study and read about those subjects we find interesting. Just as food eaten with no appetite is a tedious nourishment, so does study without zeal damage the memory by not assimilating what it absorbs. If learning is boring or dry, I even dare to say that this could damage our brains by drying them out!

All knowledge that ends in words will die quickly.

It is true, and it has been throughout my many years; like the small birds and dragonflies I studied so obsessively,

LEONARDO'S LETTER

I flitted from subject to subject as those winged creatures jump hither and yon. I still do, which is why, as I will state the obvious yet again, I am unlikely *not* to abandon this project. Unless it becomes like my Lisa, the wife of Giacondo, whose portrait I have kept with me for so many years. Paintings, as I like to say, are never completed, only abandoned. And I must say, not without a smile, that perhaps the same could be said about the story of one's life. I know that the curtain of my days will soon be drawn, and that life will abandon me. But perhaps this memoir is like that painting, one that I will keep adding to, and playing with, until I feel I get it just right.

(Or perhaps I will just dash off these silly pages and move onto something else?)

One more thing I will address before abandoning these pages for the night, as the candle sputters, and my quill is almost out of ink. It is not a pleasant question, but I will speak to it all the same.

You may be wondering, as many have, why did such a peaceful man as Leonardo allow himself to develop the tools of warfare? I am, after all, a man unable even to suffer a squawking chicken to have its neck wrung for my sustenance, so loathe was I to be the "tomb of other animals." I loved my fellow men, some would even say too much. How, then, could I design horrifying things that would destroy them in such brutal ways? How could Master Leonardo, who bought and set doves free at the market, create chariots lined with cutting knives that slice men to bits, and wicked machines to fire chunks of metal at entire armies?

I will come back to this another day, but, in short, I was curious — and needed the money.

LEONARDO'S LETTER

Amore Masculino

I have come this far, dear Cecho, so I may as well confess a bit more. What difference does it make, close as I am to death?

Soon after I moved to Florence, my body went through a kind of transformation. My voice became deep, hair grew in places that had been smooth before, and my body developed into that of a muscular and virile young man. So handsome was I, in fact, that Master Verrocchio had me pose for a statue of David, the very ideal of young manhood as he may have looked before taking on Goliath.

I confess that, around this time, I began to study myself in the mirror, and I found that I liked what I saw. Likewise, I noticed the bodies of other young men in the workshop, and I enjoyed what I saw in *them*. At first, I told myself that I apprized them as an artist must, but finally, I had to admit to myself that it went beyond simple aesthetic appreciation.

Verrocchio often had us model for the group as we studied the anatomy of the human form. While doing this, we worked at carving and painting the likenesses of each other.

I was, as many have pointed out, a great beauty in my youth. I was often chosen to pose for the other men and boys, sometimes only wearing a small loincloth, or even less.

I admit that my famous vanity grew out of this time. Simply put, I loved the attention I got. I took real joy in appreciating, even reveling in, my own beauty, knowing that it would survive through art long after it had faded in flesh.

I also slept during those years on a simple straw pallet in a dormitory reserved for the lads apprenticed like me. And, when one puts many young people of a tender age together, one cannot be surprised when certain things occur.

As you can probably guess, Cecho, several of the boys, myself included, developed infatuations. And sometimes, late at night, we would seek each other out for companionship and exploration.

I had a close relationship with several youths during that time, and Verrocchio told us that we could do whatever we wanted, so long as we were discreet and did not flaunt such actions in front of the clients of the workshop, many of whom were conservative or religious.

In fact, I think that it was almost *expected* that we artists-in-training preferred the company of other young men. It was seen as natural and normal. Of course, we generally chose not to tell our fathers or anyone outside of our circle.

I had begun to have vague feelings for other boys even earlier, but this only grew once I arrived in Florence.

I did once *try* to have a female sweetheart. I met a swarthy girl named Lucia one day as I stopped to look at the Arno while crossing the *Ponte Vecchio*. She was lively and bright, and loved to tell stories and jokes. We had a great deal of fun, if you want to know the truth, even though we were from two very different worlds.

Her father was a blacksmith. Every time I kissed her, my mind would wander from her to him, a strong man, hairy and dark, who worked bare chested in his smithy all day long. I used to steal furtive glances at him while visiting Lucia, the slick hair of his chest moistened with perspiration. I used to imagine what his sweat would smell like, and what it would feel like to kiss him, be held by him.

I had to confess to Lucia that I would never marry her. I could not tell her why, and my father was disappointed, as I think he liked her, despite her humble background. But I knew that I could never marry someone for whom I felt no attraction.

I used to feel guilty about this aspect of my life, Cecho, and I know that this is something you have struggled with as well. However, I have come to believe that God made me how I am, thus freeing me from fatherhood so that I can pursue other things.

STEVEN FARRINGTON

Lorenzo, Il Magnifico

I remember one day sometime in the early 1470s, when several of us from Verrocchio's Verrocchio workshop, including Sandro and me, were invited, along with our master, to an important event. I was seated between Master Andrea and Sandro at the banquet table of the most important person in Florence, if not all of Tuscany: Lorenzo de Medici. It was one of the great moments of my young life. It was whispered that Lorenzo wished to "study the talent" that Andrea was developing, and it was a great honor to be selected for such an occasion.

I remember feeling impressed, even a bit overwhelmed, by the beauty of the palace, although it paled in comparison to the one that would be completed years later by the official architect of the Medici, Michelozzo di Bartolomeo. Unlike the latter palace, built with the revived ideals of order and harmony absorbed from the ancients, this one, while still impressive, lacked the grace of the later structure. Still, the first level boasted glowing white marble and a great staircase leading up to what I imagined were sumptuous bedrooms and an impressive study giving onto a well-appointed library.

We were greeted at the door by an elderly servant who showed us more deference than we probably deserved as artists. As he led us through the great hall and then a narrow corridor, I marveled at the portraits of the men who had gone before Lorenzo in his family business and had built it up from a simple bank to a daunting financial empire that stretched across most of Europe. The advent of double-entry bookkeeping and letters of credit had led to this successful rise.

Though the Medici had become wealthy patrons and de facto political leaders, they had mostly used their extensive influence for good. I was about to learn about the philosophy underpinning the entire Medici project, which had been inculcated from a young age in Lorenzo, whom we now call *Il Magnifico,* as his leadership truly was magnificent.

Just before we arrived at the dining hall, well past the echoing marble staircase, we stopped before an impressive and intimidating painting of an intense-looking man staring down at us from a gilded frame.

"Who is *that*?" I asked Sandro in a quavering whisper.

"Don't you know?" Botticelli answered, also in *sotto voce*. "It's Cosimo, Lorenzo's grandfather. He's the one who had this place built. Rumor has it, young Lorenzo strives to live up to his expectations every day." He looked up at the stern and demanding man in the portrait. "It's not an easy task," he added.

Cosimo, as I was to learn later, had been *quite* the man. Educated in Latin and Greek, he was not only a scholar who collected ancient manuscripts and had founded Florence's first public library and Platonic Academy, he had also shown himself to be a shrewd and ruthless businessman.

We stood for a long moment trying to meet the gaze looking down at us, its judging eyes seeming to follow us no matter how we moved. I could hardly imagine measuring up to the expectations of such a severe man, even if I were to live *ten* lives.

"That seems like an impossible task," I said. "Just look at that fearsome brute."

"Buona sera, cari amici," came a genial voice to our left, and I was horrified to think that our host may have overheard our comments about his grandfather. But if he had, he gave no indication. Instead, he smiled and led us into a great dining room where an elaborate meal had been laid out for us.

I had mostly sworn off the eating of animal flesh by then, but I still took a bit of the roasted pheasant and picked at it just to be polite. However, I drank some of the red wine with gusto, something I rarely did, and soon, I got a bit dizzy. My tongue loosened and I felt at liberty to say whatever nonsense came to mind. This was, perhaps, because our fair-haired host was only two or three years older than me, and I just could not bring myself to see him as an authority figure, especially in the inebriated state in which I found myself. For the love of God, I had had lovers older than this lad! Back then, he was not *yet* Lorenzo *Il*

Magnifico, but seemed a callow youth, a mere heir to a fortune. This role, in my mind at least, made him seem to be in over his head.

I would see and learn much more about Lorenzo as time went on. A true athlete, he loved falconry, jousting, and breeding horses. I always wondered if he viewed us artists the same way he thought of the equines he chose shrewdly for their various characteristics. He was like a skilled chess player, and I would come to know more about his autocratic, mercenary nature, which he had likely inherited from his late grandfather.

Luckily for me, Lorenzo's later imperious character had not yet taken hold, and he was in a festive and indulgent mood that night. I was soon to learn never to doubt his intellectual heft, just as I would grow also to appreciate his business acumen.

"So, what do you plan to *do* with all of your wealth, anyway?" I asked toward the end of the meal, after the cheese and before the sweet pears were brought out for dessert.

Verrocchio kicked me under the table for the impertinence of my question, which was understandable. Medici funds had kept his workshop afloat for years.

Instead of rising in anger, Lorenzo looked amused, probably because hardly anyone approached him with such cheeky candor. A slight smile pulled at his lips as he turned to the fellow seated to his right, a blond man with brown eyes, whom he had introduced as Marsilio Fucino, his friend and tutor. The man would one day become a noted priest and intellectual, but for the moment, he was a scholar making a name for himself thanks to a translation of Aristotle from Greek into Latin. He had also been studying the only known copy of an important work of Epicurus, a work that Medici agents had miraculously discovered in a German abbey. These ancient texts had been quietly influencing the Florentine elite for years. The Medici, among others, had been commissioning art inspired by them alongside the Christian works for quite some time.

The Medici had been attempting to remake Tuscany for years, and we artists were little more than pawns in their game.

"Our philosophy is very practical and simple," Fucino said, and I laughed despite myself, earning another kick under the table, this time from Sandro.

The scholar, who by that time was well into his middle years, pretended not to notice my outburst.

"Simply put," he said, "we want to make society better through art in all its various forms."

I set my glass of wine down and stroked my then–short beard as if I were some great sage. I had not thought of art as being useful up to that point; it was just something I *did,* an activity I had to perform for various patrons. It was a practice I cared about, of course, as a *craft,* but it was not something I thought of as serving a greater purpose. I was years away, of course, from my attempted masterpiece in Milan.

Lorenzo smiled at me over his wine glass. "I am, like my father, grandfather, and uncles before me, a man on a mission," he said. "I wish to promote certain ideals through art, ideals which can improve society. Just as Marsilio here has been studying the works of the ancients and harmonizing them with Christ's teachings, so I have found a great deal of beauty and meaning in what I have read and what my tutor has been able to teach me."

"How do you mean?" I asked.

"Well, I'm glad you asked," Lorenzo said. "I'm an ambitious man, and I intend to recreate, right here in Florence, a new Athens, one based on friendship, kindness, reason, balance, and tranquility," he continued.

I looked down at my drink, not wishing to seem incredulous.

"Let us give a concrete example," Marsilio said, sensing my apprehension. "If we commission men like you to paint and sculpt works that promote calmness or beauty, that will promote those virtues, along with a sense of equanimity in the populace, and thus there will be less crime in our city, thereby making it easier to govern. Just think of it, Leonardo. What feeling comes over you when you enter the *Piazza della Signoria*, itself an aesthetic triumph, or when you contemplate the golden dome of Brunelleschi's *Duomo*, our dear Cathedral?"

I reflected for a moment. "I feel a sense of calm," I had to admit. "But even more than that, I experience pride. Yes, I feel *proud* to call myself a Florentine," I said, putting words for the first time to that feeling.

It was true. Every time I spied Florence's magnificent cathedral, which we called *Il Duomo,* thanks to Brunelleschi's great golden Dome, itself the pinnacle of art and engineering, my chest swelled with a sense of shared civic satisfaction for my city. Art and design, creativity and ingenious problem-solving…all of this was the key to Florence's success. Most of our architects were artists, and vice-versa.

I had neglected using the word "pride" for years, as my childhood tutor had warned me, on numerous occasions, of the dangers of that sin, and how it was often punished by God. However, it was true; I *did* feel proud of being a Florentine, and I said so once again.

"Well, there you are," Lorenzo said. "When you enter a public space, and you're overcome with the mathematical beauty and artistic harmony of it all, does it make men want to bandy about with swords and knives, or does it help mold them into peaceful and productive citizens?"

I had never thought about things that way before.

"And when you — and the other painters working in Verrocchio's Verrocchio stable of hand-picked talent, some might even say *genius* —" Lorenzo continued, tipping his glass in a toast to my master, who smiled and nodded in return, "when you paint a saint, or Our Lady, or Jesus, no longer as the wooden, stiff figures of the past, but now as living, breathing people, what effect does *that* have?"

I thought for a moment, the wine beginning to wear off. I was not a youth of great faith, so I had not ruminated much about this kind of thing. Finally, I said, "Well, I suppose that it leads me, and indeed, all those who experience the art, to reflect on the humanity of those biblical figures, and of our own place in the world and its stories. Perhaps they even inspire us to be better people, more like them."

"There you are again," Marsilio said. "By promoting beauty in a myriad of ways, whether through architecture, great paintings, or even by my own work of studying and translating ancient philosophy, we are creating a better society, a bit of heaven on earth, right here in Tuscany. Our own Italian brethren are doing the same up and down, from Milan to Venice, even to Naples. Soon, even Rome will be redone, and thus born again. A new Saint Peter's will be the jewel of Christendom, the envy and ornament of the world, that will stand for a thousand years. Soon, our peninsula will be the place that people from around the world will want to visit, thanks to our great artistic wonders."

I smiled, forced to admire the audacity of the vision, even as I doubted if it would work.

"Having power, my dear Leonardo," Lorenzo said, beaming like a wise teacher as he took a final sip of his wine, "is useless unless one uses it for something *worthy*. We Medici could easily retreat to our private villas, leaving Florence to public squalor while we enjoy private opulence. But *that* is not what my grandfather brought me up to do."

    I smiled. Somehow, Lorenzo seemed less young and callow to me after this supper. In fact, I thought him just the man for the daunting task he had set before himself. He would surely live up to the vision his grandfather had had for him, if not surpass it.

LEONARDO'S LETTER

The Prior

Every story needs a villain, does it not? At least, that is what Verrocchio always said, and he was a man of letters as well as a great artist.

Sadly, the villain of *my* story was all too real, far worse than any monster in a fairy tale.

I will not use my great enemy's name, as I do not wish to dignify him with any attention, even of the posthumous kind. I will simply refer to him as "The Prior," as he was the head of one of the many monasteries of Tuscany.

He was a horrible man, a hypocrite, a scoundrel, a blackmailer, and a liar. He tried many times throughout my life to have me killed, and, when that did not work, did everything in his power to deny me happiness and prosperity. Of course, I never felt safe until I learned of his death, although even that remains shrouded in doubt.

Even now, in the deepest recesses of my frequent nightmares, he rises from the grave, his face twisted in a grimace of jealous hatred, his black eyes glaring under white eyebrows and his tonsured crown, looking like a kind of evil, wasted, angry bird.

STEVEN FARRINGTON

Some of my friends thought that I had first met The Prior at one of many private parties organized by Verrocchio, the ones shrouded in darkness and secrecy, held late on moonless nights once per month, and where some Florentines probably assumed that godless rites of the occult were performed. In fact, nothing could be further from the truth; in my opinion, even though I am a humanist and a lover of *amore masculino,* nothing brought me closer to religious ecstasy in my youth than those gatherings, in which I never felt more alive, or closer to my brothers, and to the divine energy of which we are all a part.

Verrocchio organized several such parties in the fall of 1475 and during that winter. Since it was Florence, the city of artists, these parties were well attended, although every man who came was sworn to secrecy, and this system usually worked quite well. Our code for ourselves was *"finocchio,"* as we had the finest eyes for things of beauty.

As many of us partook in the immoderate imbibing of wine at such parties, we fancied ourselves as the inheritors of the ancient god Bacchus. We began calling our festivals *bacchanalia,* and instead of exclaiming to God, saying *Oddio*, or *per Dio*, as our mothers and priests did, we took to exclaiming *perbacco* amongst one another. We saw Bacchus as our true and favorite deity, our own private patron saint.

To enter the party each month, each man would whisper the secret code: *Tre, tre, uno, tre, tre* — three, three, one, three, three. More on this later, although anyone reading this would understand why we chose this combination.

We from the artists' guild knew who was safe to invite to such evenings, and everyone who came understood the need for absolute discretion, despite how open-minded Florence was. And the men who were married and loved women in our milieu were generally understanding about fellows like us. Some of them even preferred having us as friends above all others, knowing that we were unlikely to pursue their wives and sweethearts. I daresay that we made better companions for them than most of their mates, who only wanted to drink and fight in low taverns; we were the ones who cared about them, and, if necessary, would even comfort them in times of need.

In any case, I remember the first time I spied The Prior, and it was *not* at one of these parties. Instead, just as I would meet my beloved muse Lisa at the market, so did I first lay eyes on my great enemy at that very same place.

I understood from the first that he was a prior, in charge of some monastery. I will never understand why he didn't simply allow the cook or kitchen manager to do his shopping for him, but there he was, examining the produce. I just remember him looking up as we locked eyes, and I understood instantly what he wanted. I later heard that he craved young men like me, especially those with golden eyes and light brown or blond curls.

I kept walking, trying not to look at him. Of course, I never cast aside the idea of an older lover *a priori* (no pun intended). But the idea of a man who was clearly dressed as the leader of a religious order? I knew, even at *that* tender age, that such a thing could only bring problems.

If only I'd known *what* problems!

Soon, every time I was out and about, but usually at the market, I would find the man waiting and watching. Sometimes, he would even follow me. It was both uncanny — how did he track my movements? — and profoundly disturbing. I would even vary the days I visited the market, but somehow, he always seemed to know when I would be there.

One day, he pursued me into an alley off the *Piazza della Signoria*, just a few steps away from the box into which he would soon deposit his anonymous accusation. How bold he was, hunting me like that so near our city's center of power. How protected he must have felt by his status as a religious leader.

Finally, one day, I had had enough.

"What? What is it that you want of me?" I demanded, turning on him, visibly startling the man. His head bobbed over a brown frock upon which a large cross had been embroidered in red. Even then, the slim fringe of his hair had turned white, and a sea of wrinkles sank his black eyes into deep sockets.

"I, em…" he said, struggling for words. "I am always on the lookout for young men who might like to join my order," he said, when it was clear that I wasn't interested in letting him suck my *cazzo*. "Would you be interested in joining as a novice?"

I wondered if this line had ever actually worked for him, or if it were just some kind of code of which I was unaware.

"No, thank you," I said, raising my chin in a defiant gesture. "I am a man of the arts, a humanist of Verrocchio's workshop, and I have no interest in becoming a man of the cloth."

I saw his ruined face light up with understanding. I realized that I should not have told him where I worked, nor who I was associated with. It was also unfortunate that Verrocchio rhymed with *finocchio*.

"I was led to understand that men like you were often given to, well...a certain need...to confess their many sins," he said. "If ever you need to relieve yourself of any burden, my son, you need only to call."

"Don't waste my time," I said, trying to brush past him, and I almost had to pry one of his ancient claws from my smock as I struggled to get away.

Months later, I saw him at one of our secret gatherings, around Easter. I was beyond surprised to see him there. I felt horrified that he had been able to penetrate the sanctum of this most secret Florentine society. He was dressed as a wool merchant, with fresh hose and a red tunic.

That night, Verrocchio had hired Jacopo Saltarelli, a handsome young apprentice goldsmith and sometime model for the studio. Of course, that night, he had been paid to provide services other than simply modeling.

The Prior spent the entire evening perched alone in a corner. No one spoke to him, and this was not because of his advanced age. Other old men sometimes attended, and they were often more popular than the young, thanks to their great skills and experience. But this time, the old crow sat neglected off to the side. Even Jacopo refused to touch him.

And so it was, dear Cechino, that less than a week later, a letter denouncing your Leonardo and several other men of sodomy was slipped into the *tamburo* of the city hall in the *Piazza della Signoria*.

Luckily, no proof was ever given, the letter was unsigned, and no witnesses ever corroborated the denunciation. Thank God that my friend Leonardo Tornabuoni had friends in high places, and he was able to use his influence to get us out of jail once we had been locked up. It was also whispered, I don't know by whom, that we were Masons, which, although suspect, was less bad than being considered sodomites. I suppose this rumor would explain, to those who wished to believe it, our alleged practice of secret meetings.

However, the fact remained that *someone* from our secret society had denounced us.

I had no proof, but in my heart of hearts, I always knew who had done it. I only wondered how the man had gained access to the secret code, who had been foolish enough to give it to him.

The damage to my career and reputation had been done, and I would never forgive the man I still call only "The Prior."

Un Primo Amore

After some time of dissipation in those early years, I am happy to say that I finally fell in love, around the time of my thirtieth birthday.

(Please, Cecho, don't be jealous. No one will ever be your equal in my heart!)

As anyone who knows me may guess, my first true love was none other than a man with whom I shared a bedchamber and a workspace off and on for many years, so it was only natural that we should fall in love:

Sandro.

Of course it was Sandro! We spent so much time together, and by 1481 or so, when he returned from a stint in the Vatican, we decided to make a try at being a couple.

We had an agreement always to be truthful to each other, without any expectations of fidelity; indeed, until my later years, I was always a man of great appetites, and though Sandro wished me to be faithful, he knew my limitations in this regard.

Sandro said that he accepted me as I was, but I knew he was lying. Even though he had numerous peccadillos himself, this didn't prevent him from judging mine. He threw frequent fits of rage and jealousy, of course, and we would fight for hours before making up and then making love all night long. This happened again and again in a vicious and dramatic cycle.

Despite this, however, we experienced a great first love, the kind that only young men who feel free and have their whole lives ahead of them can share.

I have no regrets.

I still remember the night that Sandro and I became intimate. We had been out drinking in various taverns, only to end up on the bank of the Arno, gazing up at the moon. He began telling me about an idea he had had for a masterpiece for the new Medici palace. It would be an allegory about the rebirth of the human spirit after a long winter of barrenness, which he would call *Primavera*.

While in Rome, he had devoured several of the ancient works that Lorenzo had instructed us all to read, such as the *De Rerum Nature* by Titus Lucretius Carus. This, among other readings, had inspired my friend to make a painting for Lorenzo, he said, and it would make his name famous for centuries.

"What will it be of?" I asked. I had truly missed my friend during his absence, and his enthusiasm for art and ideas was infectious.

"Well," he said, brushing his brown hair away from his face, "it will be of Venus in her garden, inviting the viewer in," he began. "As the goddess of love, she will beckon us to enter and experience love, along with Zephyrus, the god of wind, who falls in love with Chloris, turning her into Flora, complete with a garden of eternal spring and fertility."

"I like the idea of eternal fertility," I said, moving closer to him at the water's edge and lightly placing a hand on his thigh. Sandro cast a look at me that showed that he both disapproved of what I was implying, but also didn't entirely want me to stop.

"And then, I plan to place Mercury, the god of reason, at the other side of the painting," he continued. "This way, he can direct the viewer toward another companion piece outside of the painting, sending a message of neo-platonic love. Virtue over lust," he concluded.

I moved even closer to my friend. "I'm not sure I can support *that*," I said, taking an obvious chance. "Sometimes we need to cast virtue aside and embrace a healthy expression of lust," I whispered.

"Yes, perhaps, *sometimes*," my friend said with a gulp, clearly trying to control himself. I had begun gently to caress Sandro's manhood under his light tunic. "But only occasionally. Only in moderation."

"Of course," I whispered, drawing my mouth closer to his ear. "Tell me about the other painting."

"Which other one?" Alessandro said, his voice cracking. I could tell it had been months since he'd allowed himself to indulge in the masculine love that was so rampant in Florence. Still, even though I knew it would be easy to bed him, I knew of the fun and delight that came from seducing a man through art. And this was not just *any* man. This was Sandro Botticelli, for whom I had developed strong feelings over several years.

"Tell me about your companion piece," I whispered. "The one that Mercury will aim his bow at."

"Oh, that one will be a favorite piece," he said, and I loved to hear my friend speak so, the passion of his project exciting him as much as the prospect of sex. Perhaps even more.

"Tell me about it," I said, my lips brushing his earlobe and gently nuzzling his neck.

"Well, this one will feature Minerva, the goddess of wisdom, and she will be dominating…" his voice trailed off, a look of desire inflaming his eyes as he turned to look at me directly in the moonlight.

"Yes?" I asked, letting the word hover in the air with a note of expectation.

"In this painting, she will dominate a centaur," he finished. I could tell that he was losing his battle for composure.

"How appropriate," I said. "A creature that is half-man, half-beast, being held by the hair," I said, gently reaching up to play with my friend's light-brown mane and grasping it in a way that was both gentle and slightly dominant.

"The perfect submission of passion to wisdom," I said. "And let me guess. Minerva will arrest this beast *before* he can shoot his arrow, yes? Will that be the way of it?"

Sandro could barely conceal the desire in his eyes. His entire body ached for pleasure and release. He slowly nodded, unable to speak.

"Perhaps the poor centaur has been wanting to shoot his arrow for so long, and now that he can't do so, he doesn't know what else to do," I said.

I took him by the hand and led him back to my room. We lit candles and I seduced my friend a bit more. Before finally taking him, I whispered, "Sometimes the centaur *wants* to be caught, doesn't he?"

To this, Sandro gyrated and nodded with gusto, a smile on his lips, and I knew exactly what he desired.

LEONARDO'S LETTER

Il Corpo Umano (The Human Body)

On Master Andrea's suggestion, I presented myself to the medics and monks of Santa Maria's hospice. At first, the idea of studying human anatomy disgusted me. Soon, however, it would become one of my life's greatest passions. In fact, Cecho, instead of writing this foolish narrative, I certainly *should* be compiling all my findings into a folio treatise based on what I have learned in over forty years of human dissection. Please put one together for me if I die before I get around to that, will you, dear boy?

In any case, Verrocchio knew one of the surgeons at the hospice, and I was allowed to study the corpses of the recently deceased, provided that I helped with some of the unpleasant tasks of the place, such as emptying out the chamber pots and washing the patients with rags dipped in water. When doing this, I placed a bandage dipped in vinegar around my face, or sometimes strapped a mask with pleasant-smelling herbs in front of my mouth. I had to do this for about a month before they allowed me to take a scalpel to any dead flesh.

I remember the first time I was allowed to dissect a human body. How can anyone forget something like that?

He was a young man, not much older than me, a father who had been stricken with an unknown illness that had made him lose weight quickly. I remember when he was first brought into the hospice; he was a handsome man, a friendly sort that we Florentines would call *un ragazzo fico,* so pleasant was his company. His name was Filippo and I spent hours talking to him. His wife and daughter would visit him every day, but toward the end, they were naturally there all the time until he passed.

His final wish, he told his wife, as well the priest who gave him last rites, was to allow me to dissect his body to learn about what had killed him. Of course, this would be right before his family would hold a vigil for him and then wrap him in a burial shroud.

I was to be given one night to learn as much as I could about him, and an elderly physician would assist me as I cut him open.

I will never forget that night as long as I live.

The old physician, who had studied in Bologna and had even been to the Sorbonne in Paris, had me begin with an incision in Filippo's lower stomach, which had become bloated in recent months. I held my breath as I cut into the flesh that had so recently been alive.

I noticed that the blood didn't flow as strongly as it did when we bled living patients (a practice I doubt serves any real purpose). I continued to cut until I reached the man's intestines, which reminded me of the "trippa" that I had observed in the animals of my mother's farm village when they were slaughtered. The idea that we humans might just be a creature like any other crossed my mind, and this both fascinated and scared me. What if we were not a unique creation, but rather little more than beasts with brains?

Soon after sifting through the tripes of the man, we finally came to what we were looking for. Doctor Federico reached in with some metal pincers, wincing all the while, and pulled out a disgusting black chunk that was almost as big as a fist.

"Here it is," he said, throwing it down on the slab next to Filippo's body with an audible *thwap*. "There's the tumor," the doctor said. "That's what killed him."

I stared in disbelief at the mound of putrid rottenness that had taken my friend's life.

What could have happened to make that horrible thing form and grow? And could it ever be prevented? I had so many questions.

"Porca miseria!" the older man spat. "The problem with poor Filippo is that he didn't come in when this whole thing started," the doctor said. "His humors were all out of balance. If only I could have bled him adequately, starting, say, eight months ago, none of this would have happened, and he'd still be alive today."

I stared in disbelief at the doctor, and then down again at the tumor and my friend's lifeless body.

There had to be some other explanation, I thought. And *perbacco,* I was going to find out what it was!

LEONARDO'S LETTER

Trouble and Travel

Many have scoffed at my lifelong habit of avoiding the flesh of animals — as I have said many times, I never wanted to be the tomb of another living creature. Throughout my studies, I found that I am not alone; many of the ancients, such as Pythagoras, also eschewed the eating of meat. I was even able to convince some of my students and lovers to avoid meat, and I would love to make a long-term study to see if such a practice can prolong life, as is my suspicion. I am now a man almost to the age of seventy, and have long outlived both my parents and my uncle, so maybe there's something to this idea.

Of course, many would say that my care and compassion for lowly beasts was sorely misplaced during such a time of war and strife.

There were, indeed, so many problems plaguing our Italian states during those years. The Medici were always involved in some imbroglio or other, and the Borgias seemed intent on outdoing each other in their unquenchable thirst for power. We were threatened on every side; Aragon and Castile were flexing their muscles, the Mamalook Turks and the French wanted to swallow us up, and lest any future reader imagine that Italy was united, Naples wanted to strike Tuscany. Also, dangerous clouds were gathering within Florence itself.

Therefore, it was good that I was sent, as part of a diplomatic mission, to that fortress of a city whose leader, Ludovico Sforza, known as "Il Moro," made Milan seem like something like a peaceful haven.

But before jumping to Milan, I have more to say about my time in the Tuscan capital. One specific conversation is important to mention here, and it happened while I was shopping for materials to use for dyes and paints.

Part of the lore surrounding me was that while visiting various markets of Florence, I would purchase birds and release them, smiling as I watched them fly away. To be honest, I can only remember doing this a few times.

One day, after buying some eggs, vinegar, linseeds, and poppies for tempera, my eyes fell on a perfectly beautiful white dove cooing in her cage. I was overcome with compassion for her. I also wanted to study how she flew, obsessed as I was by the subject of flight. I plunked down a few coins, took the lively white bird in my hands, and chuckled as I watched her head bob this way and that as she struggled against my gentle hold. Little did she know I was her liberator, about to set her free! A moment later, I tossed her into the air and saw her take flight and escape into the blue, cloudless sky.

"Perhaps you could find a better use for your time, my boy," came a voice from behind me. I turned, wondering if it were The Prior, come to torment me again, but instead, I saw a man I hadn't seen for quite some time: my father!

LEONARDO'S LETTER

Most men would give their fathers an embrace or perhaps a kiss on the cheek, but this was not the way between my *pater* and me. Instead, he shook my hand as if I were nothing more than a merchant he had once met, and told me that he'd been following my progress and that he hoped I could put my talents toward something useful.

"What do you mean, Father?" I asked.

"I haven't forgotten, you know," he replied, a wry smile on his lips. "You are not only a talented artist, my son, but you are also clever in *all* your designs, or so Verrocchio has told me. Perhaps you could draw up means of defense, or even ways for cities to *attack* one another," he said. "Let me see what I can do. Ludovico, the Moor, was quite impressed with your shield years ago," he said with a wink. "I hear that he's been asking after your other talents as well."

I felt torn. I did not relish the idea of devising ways for men to kill or injure one another, but there was another side, the engineer in me, that was intrigued. Despite my gentle spirit that recoiled even at the death of animals, I later became, at the court of Ludovico, and later still of Cesare Borgia, a talented designer of the machines of war.

Please know this, Cecho: for me, with everything I tried, I was hardly *ever* concerned with the finished product of my labors, at least while devising them. My mind was absorbed in the creative process and the delight of discovery. Such was my thirst for knowledge, my endless curiosity, that the journey of carrying any project to fruition was such an intense pleasure that I could go for weeks barely sleeping, keeping such strange hours that I was hardly seen.

I designed flying machines based on the wings of bats and birds. I formed plans for covered vehicles, huge cannons, and monstrous crossbows capable of wiping out entire armies. I filled notebook after notebook with projects I will leave for others to complete once I am gone. For me, these were personal challenges I relished just as much as that three-year project I did in Milan, *The Last Supper*, for which I studied geometry, philosophy, religion, anatomy, and so much more. It was a work of such power that the abbot of the monastery fell to his knees before the fresco, so overcome was he. Why use false modesty now? I am far too old for that!

It is true; a painting is only ever abandoned. That is why my favorite piece, my mistress, the only woman I have ever truly loved, is a lady I have carried from place to place, and she has ended up here with us in Amboise. I could never finish nor abandon her, not even now, as the angel of death approaches and I can almost smell his breath on my neck.

And what of my time in the court of Ludovico? Was I hired as a court engineer and military strategist?

Sadly, no. No, my main task at Ludovico's court was something so frivolous that I feel almost ashamed to mention it here.

I was hired for the planning of an endless series of senseless celebrations. Such was, I suspect, the *true* reason he hired me and kept me on; it is well-known that men such as I are good at creating fantastic and fabulous performances that amuse and evoke joy and merriment. The lavish festivities I produced are too numerous to name, but I promise to revisit these later if I persist with this project. For now, I will only say that I may have begun simply as a designer of pageants, but I threw myself into them to make them more meaningful, at least to me. I poured all my creativity into that work, and I did my best to infuse a bit of the awe I felt for the world, and our place in it, into those spectacles.

Men of lofty genius, I often say, when they are doing the least work, are the most active. So if this is true, then the reverse must *also* be true. Even though I relished my time at Ludovico's court, it was among the least productive times of my life.

Was I born to create pageants and other ephemera? I highly doubt it.

I had many varied wanderings over the years following the French invasion of Milan. And of course, I returned there years later to find great happiness, which shows that life rarely turns out the way we expect.

After the fall of Milan, I hoped to live in the delightful city of Mantua with my dear friend Cecilia, whom I had known as Il Moro's mistress years before, but that was never meant to be. Her mistress, the great humanist Isabella d'Este Gonzaga, could not allow me to stay. I can hardly blame her; her fragile state of Mantua could have fallen if King Louis had decided to strike, and rumor had it that he sought a pretext to do just that. Apparently, even my minor celebrity and talent was known to the French. Hiding me might have served as such a pretext for the French, and Isabella could never allow such a thing.

Ah, Isabella! I could write for weeks about that woman. I shall never forget the scant time I spent with her at the end of 1499. I appeared on a day when diplomats arrived from nearby Venice, where her husband, Francesco of Gonzaga, had lately been on a state visit. I remember several of us crowded into her *studiolo*, where the Venetians and I stood gasping for breath in the dusty air and looking up at Andrea Montegna's painting of some scene by Ovid, a shaft of morning sun illuminating a Daphne transformed into a laurel tree as Apollo pursued her.

While most women in her position collected religious art, if anything, Isabella adored anything from the Ancient World. She relished mythology and old stories, and even read Ovid in Latin, which she claimed to do poorly, but I knew better. During my brief stay, I was able to inspect her library, and I can assert that her collection was quite impressive.

I recall a large stack of letters and quills on her writing desk. Rumors of her correspondence and a vast network of friends, to whom she wrote back and forth in several languages, seemed true.

I remember how, when her servant whispered of my desire to speak to her in private, she made some excuse and glided out of the *studiolo* to walk with me in her courtyard and talk alone. Before asking after the situation in Milan, she made me promise to sketch her, which I did, so much was I taken with her. It's true, no one could refuse a request from Isabella. That is, of course, until I declined to paint her years later, but that's another story.

"And where do you intend to go now, *maestro*?" she asked, perching on a bench beside a small pond and indicating that I should sit across from her. Of course, she knew my nature, and was always comfortable around me, even being alone with me for hours at a time.

"Well, to be frank, *signora*, I would love it if I could perhaps…stay here for a while."

The spark went out from her lively dark eyes as she looked down into her lap, her lovely white hands resting on a blue gown under a green bodice. Even her gold turban seemed to droop a bit on her mane of fiery red hair.

"We shall see, my friend," she said evasively, and I knew better than to insist. Her situation was obviously precarious, and Mantua was always her main priority.

A close second, however, was promoting the arts in her court. Not only did she patronize painters, like the fortunate Montegna, but also poets, musicians, minstrels, ceramic artists, translators, and artists who created medals made of brass, bronze, and gold stamped with her likeness. I am proud that she gave me one of these, once my cartoon of her was complete.

There are many who have since spoken of an uncanny resemblance of that sketch with a painting I did later in Venice, a replica, and the one I did of Lisa. What no one knows, although I imagine a few may suspect, is that I always thought of my old friend Isabella when I painted that portrait. This, I did only for myself.

Oh, if only I could have stayed there! I would have made the perfect courtier for Mantua. I would have painted her as well as everyone else at her court. I may even have become a poet. However, life took another turn, which is doubtless for the best. Like a sailor for siren songs long ago, I would have crashed upon that coast, or become a lazy lotus-eater, and who would *that* have helped?

I also hoped, for a time, to live in the glorious city of Venice. How could anyone with eyes and a heart not fall in love with *La Serenissima*? That most serene city of canals and sloping bridges made me almost weep just by walking around her. The sunlight as it dappled the dark blue water, the luminous white and gray of her palazzos, the sight of her muscular young men as they competed in their yearly regatta, the idea of riding as a guest of honor in the prow, made my heart sing with joy. However, life pulled me to Rome where I became a pawn in the Borgia papal court, then back again to Florence where my rivalry with that upstart Michelangelo would become the stuff of legend.

Atalante

It is true what they say. Many handsome and talented men drifted in and out of my life before I met you, my Cecho. Sandro was my *inamorato* for a while, but after a time, we went back to being friends. My life as an artist continued to progress, but I didn't come to be famous overnight, hindered as I was in my work life by the blow dealt by The Prior. Once I had established myself in Florence, and word spread about the kind of man I am, the disciples found me, whether I sought them out or not.

One such example is, in fact, one of my favorites, Atalante Migliorotti. He was my enchanting companion for about ten years until around the time I adopted Salaì, and he followed me from Tuscany to the court of Milan.

I remember well meeting him. I was almost thirty, and the first wisps of gray were creeping into my beard. I was still part of Andrea Verrocchio's Verrocchio workshop, although I had my own workspace by then. If I remember correctly, I was there that day to discuss the effects of light and perspective, and how best to design a fresco before setting brush to canvas. I had honed techniques for applying the principles of mathematics for maximum effect that I would later use for *The Last Supper* in Milan. I was also on my way to gaining expertise in human anatomy, and had been doing experiments with several young men, having them stand just so at various times of day while the light entered my studio window at differing angles. Soon, after speaking to Verrocchio and a few others, I noticed a shy, handsome boy of perhaps nineteen sitting on a bench to my left. He didn't speak, but rather seemed to watch me as I held forth.

I remember thinking that I would very much like to do a study of his face. There was a firm line to his jaw, a slightly jutting chin, a light blond mustache, curls the way I like, and enchanting dark eyes that held just a touch of mischief. I also imagined how the afternoon light might strike what I guessed were toned muscles on a supple body. Yes, I decided, I could very much enjoy spending some time with this lad. For the sake of art, of course.

After some time, the other artists began to drift back to their own projects. Soon I found myself alone with the graceful young man, who, despite his poor station in life, wore red hose and a green ruby-edged doublet. This was a gift, I learned later, of a bishop whose assistant he had been for a while, until the wagging tongues of Florence forced the older man to end the friendship.

Let us not forget, Florence was among the most indulgent places in Christendom, but even she had her limits. Despite the city's tolerance, there was one figure who was beginning to cast a pall over everyone and everything, one who made The Prior seem a saint in comparison: Girolamo Savonarola. We all feared no one more than that fanatical Dominican whose fiery predications echoed from his cursed pulpit. His reign of terror made even the least sinful of the Tuscan capital quake with fear.

"I am here to seek help from Verrocchio," the young man explained. I engaged him in conversation and soon learned that his name was Atalante. Like me, he was the fruit of an illegitimate union. His mother had played at trying to outrun the boy's father before allowing herself to be caught as he pursued her among the hedges of an orchard, the gales of laughter causing her almost to lose her voice. She had finally, and against her better judgment, yielded to the dapper courtier in a moment of unbridled lust inside a private bedchamber at one of the Medici palazzos, where she worked as a nurse to Lorenzo the Magnificent. Due to her constant presence at the boy's side, she always heard his tutors drone on and on about the stories of Antiquity, and had become, in spite of herself, an educated woman. Thus, when she had her son around 1463, she named him after the Greek legend of a maiden who had promised never to marry unless a man could run as swiftly as she. Who said it couldn't be a boy's name as well?

However, unlike your Leonardo, who had been raised with care despite my illegitimate status, Atalante had had no such luck. He had been passed off to poor relations in Fiosole, where he helped his aunt as a cheese vendor in a local market until he escaped to the quarters of Bishop Quadrini, hidden in plain sight as the man's personal valet.

"My previous protector always enjoyed hearing me sing," the boy said, brushing one of his blond curls behind an ear under a red cap. "I was hoping that, perhaps, Master Leonardo, you could teach me to sing properly, as they say that you excel at every art known to man."

"Well, I don't know if *that's* true," I began, but the lad looked at me with his soft and knowing brown eyes, which were full of insight, even for one so young. Those eyes seemed to say that false modesty was both unnecessary and beneath me. I studied the young man's fine, long fingers.

"Have you ever considered stroking the lyre?" I asked. "Or perhaps the lute?"

At this, the boy only smiled.

"I have never even seen a lyre up close. I wouldn't know where to begin."

"Why don't you come back with me? I have a lovely silver one, and I would be happy to teach you. Plus, I could use an assistant." I paused. "That is, if you've nowhere to live or if you seek employment." This was several years before I met the impish Salaì. And while my mind harbored little doubt about what this lad was about, the danger posed by Savonarola and his ilk forced men such as I always to dance around the subject, speaking in fanciful codes and oblique offers that could be rescinded if necessary.

"Go back with you?" the boy said, pausing, appearing to think the matter over for a long moment. "Yes.

That would be lovely," he finally replied, as if this had been his plan all along.

And as far as I know, it had been. I never asked, preferring to think of this as a serendipitous meeting that changed both our lives for the better for several years to come.

Naturally, the boy became my special friend, and eventually, of course, my lover. Why deny it? I am practically on my deathbed, and I hope that you will not become inflamed with jealousy and decide to burn these pages in a hot-tempered fit of anger, my love. However, my Cecho is nothing if not understanding and kind, and you may simply hide these pages in one of my codices. Although, it's not like I haven't already spoken of my proclivities...

In any case, Atalante was an ideal companion. For several years, he went everywhere with me. Not only did I teach him all I knew about architecture, anatomy, and mathematics, but also how to read music and to speak passable Latin and French. Under my tutelage, he learned how to dress, and I taught him how to sing and act properly, how to enchant ladies and cultivate the favor of powerful men. And, of course, I taught him to play both the lute *and* the lyre. He would accompany me north the following year, and he was quite a success at the Sforza court. Oh yes, the handsome fellow did well by attaching himself to me, if I do say so without boasting.

STEVEN FARRINGTON

One of my favorite possessions is a sketch I have of Atalante. It is, no doubt, buried somewhere in my trunks or boxes. It shows him with his face upturned while listening to some finches singing outside our parlor window one September day. His eyes gleamed as one completely in love with the world, and, as I remember it, he looked as if composing in his mind a piece for the lyre that would imitate the birdsong. A ray of light from the window shone on the irises of his eyes, the pupils constricting, and I was overcome with emotion. I could hardly resist trying to capture him with my charcoal chalk.

Years later, I began an oil painting of him on a small walnut panel, several of which someone at court had given me for portraits. I spent over a month getting his face just right, but had to abandon the project, as Ludovico demanded my attention for the planning of an extravagant spectacle for an ambassador visiting from somewhere or other. Having to coordinate so many troubadours, design sets and pulleys, prepare music and dances, and come up with representations of gods and celestial bodies took so much out of me that I left the portrait to be completed by one of my protégés, whose name I cannot recall. I had captured Atalante's graceful face for posterity, however, as he gazed into a strong light. What did I care if a lesser artist put him in a stiff brown doublet and black tunic? His face glowed all the more for that! The fact that he holds sheet music is one detail that I insisted upon, of course. I wanted everyone to know how important Atalante the Musician was, at least to me. It is, of course, the only painting I've ever done of a man. This was years before I met Lisa, *La Gioconda*.

It has been a long time since I saw my young friend, but I believe that fortune has smiled on him, and that he is currently in Rome helping the Medici to build new Saint Peter's. Perhaps he has even become Michelangelo's lover, if he can stand being around that annoying, crass, selfish carver.

STEVEN FARRINGTON

La Volta, or The Prior's Return

Things were going well for me; I was working, earning good commissions, and enjoying my time with Atalante. Sadly, life has taught me that, when such moments appear, something always comes along and spoils things.

I was at the market when I felt his cloying presence behind me. The malefic intentions the man always held were palpable in a way that I have never known how to explain.

The Prior.

I turned to face him, trying to sound brave. "What is it that you want this time?" I demanded.

"I just wanted to ask you a question, my boy," he said, taking a step closer. "Have you ever read the book of Matthew?"

This was a silly question, I thought. One did not just sit down and *read* the Bible. It was read to people in church, and then priests would explain the passage, usually in Latin, saying what it meant to those attending Mass. Everyone knew that.

"Do you remember the parable of the wheat and the weeds?" he asked.

I shook my head. My old tutor back in Vinci had gone on about the Bible, but this story did not stand out in my memory.

"Well," the old prior said, drawing uncomfortably close, so near in fact that I could smell his rotten breath, "the short version of it is that God has sown good seed in the world, represented by the wheat, but Satan has come to sow weeds among the crops. And so, in the end, the weeds will be separated from the wheat, even if it takes time."

"So, what has that got to do with *me*?" I asked, trying to hide my fear.

"And do you know what will happen to the weeds, those found unworthy of God's love? Those who have given in to temptation and not lived according to God's plan? Or those who have sinned, but then not been pardoned by a holy man? You know, Leonardo," he said, reaching out and caressing my cheek with one of his skeletal fingers, "if you were to sin with *me*, for example, I could immediately give you penance, thus wiping the slate clean. It would be as if the sin had never happened."

I drew back, trying in vain to get away, but he had me against a wall.

"But if, in the end, you are found to be one of the impure weeds," he said in a whisper so low it was almost a hiss, "you will be thrown into the furnace, where there will be weeping and gnashing of teeth!"

"I can see no greater punishment than spending time with you," I said, escaping the old man's grasp and darting away into the alley.

"You say that now!" he called after me. "Someday, you will regret defying me! I have friends in high places!"

Luckily, I did not know then how close I came to facing the flames and tortures of which The Prior spoke.

LEONARDO'S LETTER

Lorenzo's Emissary

Not long after this terrifying encounter, and mere months after meeting Atalante, I was summoned to a special audience with Lorenzo *il Magnifico*. He was really starting to live up to that sobriquet by then, and his vision for our city was starting to bear fruit. Palatial palaces were springing up all over Florence by then, and his *palazzo* was the best of all. It grew more regally opulent with each passing year.

I had received the summons to his palace by a messenger clad in the finest hose and doublet, and the note I received was polite but terse, letting me know, in no uncertain terms, that turning down the invitation to the Medici palace was most definitely *not* an option.

Of course, I feared that this could have something to do with The Prior, but then Verrocchio's Verrocchio secretary assured me that I was not in danger. In fact, he assured me with a wink, this meeting was about my future. Lorenzo was sending artists abroad to represent him. Perhaps I was to fill the void of some fortunate painter sent to Venice or Rome. If I were lucky, Lorenzo might have plans involving greater commissions around Florence, ones that the Prior would be unable to prevent me from obtaining. If fortune smiled on me, perhaps I would be sent to the

Vatican to decorate some of the private rooms of the Borgia pope, Alexander.

It was only then that I thought back to the chance meeting with my father in the market. Had he been corresponding with influential people on my behalf, or advocating for me when notarizing documents for Lorenzo? Perhaps, I thought. He was, of course, the notary of many important people around the city and beyond. Maybe I would be sent to Mantua, or somewhere close like Faenza, Siena, or Assisi.

Atalante came along with me for this *tête-à-tête,* and he gave me a playful nudge when we passed the bedchamber where he suspected he had been conceived. We shared a private laugh at this detail, one of many moments of shared complicity. I had hoped to catch sight of my lover's mother, whom Atalante saw rarely, but this was not to be.

There was one person who *did* catch my eye, however, as I glanced out an open window; he was a young boy, covered in sweat and marble dust as he worked on some rudimentary statue. When I asked Atalante who he was, I detected a note of jealousy when he explained that this gifted dark-haired lad was none other than Michelangelo Buonarroti, who would later become my rival. I believe that Atalante imagined what the boy would look like years later, and perhaps feared that he could usurp his own position.

He needn't have worried.

I was surprised that Atalante was allowed to go in with me, and soon, we were shown into what amounted to Lorenzo's throne room, although the man simply sat behind a large chestnut desk. He got right to the point, as he usually did, having grown blunter in his advancing age.

"I've been sending out various artists to help me shore up Florence's influence and relations with other states on the peninsula," he said, without preamble. "Verrocchio is bound for Venice, and Botticelli heads back to Rome to curry favor with the pope. The Borgias are so unpredictable, I need to have my best man there to keep an eye on things."

He paused, as if to let the fact that I was decidedly *not* his best man sink in for a moment. "I'd like to send *you* on an extended trip to the Duchy of Milan, Leonardo," he concluded. "You shall plan parties and celebrations for The Moor, Ludovico, the regent, who is a Duke in all but name only."

My heart sank, and my first thought, upon hearing this, was that I didn't *want* to be sent away to that northern city. The Milanese had a horrible reputation in those days, which, even though I grew eventually to love them, I admit is not completely undeserved.

Also, I was an artist, a gifted one at that, someone who could design all manner of useful and interesting things. Why would I want to waste my time designing pageants and parties for a ducal court?

"But, Your Excellency, surely there may be a better use of my—"

"It's not a mere *request*," Lorenzo said, leaning forward, his gray eyes narrowing almost to slits under a wrinkled brow. "You *will* do as I ask. Men like you only serve to plan parties and celebrations," he said with a wave of his hand.

I began to understand that The Prior, and perhaps others, had told him about the kind of man I was, a mere *finocchio,* and this had led Lorenzo to overlook my many other talents.

Of course, even though I am ashamed now to admit it, I was sorry in that moment to have brought Atalante along with me, both because having him by my side only reinforced my nature in my patron's mind, and because I hated being humiliated in front of my lover.

"Go home, *Master* Leonardo," he said, the sarcasm almost dripping off his lips. "Go home and think it over. I want to loan you out to Ludovico, the Moor, but if you refuse…know that I can make life difficult for you."

A lump formed in my throat. The 1476 accusation stood out in my mind. Atalante and I had been careful, but there was no doubt that *Il Magnifico* knew the truth. Medici spies were everywhere. Lorenzo wouldn't think twice about tossing me into prison, sending me to the gallows, or worse, for nothing at all. Then again, he could perhaps see to it that I would be denied jobs, or that my workshop failed in ways hard to prove. His advisor, Machiavelli, would counsel him against any outright sabotage, especially if he stood to gain nothing from such a move. The Medici were shrewd, after all, but Lorenzo was not a king, as Florence was technically still a republic. The Medici had held power for generations operating behind the scenes whenever possible.

Even though Lorenzo was powerful, proper channels had to be followed, and the delegates who met at the *Palazzo Della Signoria* would never let him do whatever he wanted. Despite his influence, he did not have a total *carte blanche.*

I bowed deeply to Lorenzo, and Atalante did the same. We took our leave, promising to send an answer by courier within the week.

Atalante and I discussed our strategy late into the night. On the one hand, I loved Florence. Nevertheless, did I perhaps want to spread my wings and fly, like the doves at the market? Did I not feel like a bird trapped in a cage? Had I not been complaining about such a feeling for months?

Residing in the same city as The Prior felt like living under the Sword of Damocles, which could fall at any moment. This was without even *mentioning* the growing religious fanaticism in our fair republic.

Milan had no Savonarola. That was a point in its favor.

And yet...what did I *really* know of Milan? I called some friends over to the workshop, and while the wine flowed freely, we discussed various things we knew about that place.

Milan was three times the size of Florence, as one friend pointed out. The city was crisscrossed with a network of canals, and scores of mills and silkworm factories had transformed the city into a capital of both fashion and industry. Atalante's ears pricked up upon hearing this, as the bishop and I had clearly spoiled him with expensive hose and doublets, and the idea of living in such a place obviously appealed to him.

The thing that clinched it for me, however, was when my friend Giovanni told me of how Ludovico, known as *il moro,* thanks to his dark complexion that made him look like a man from the lands of Araby, had created a lavish court full of the brightest minds of northern Italy.

"Milan's court is just the place for you, Master Leonardo," the boy said, his dark curls dancing playfully. "You can be yourself there, nobody will care where you put your *cazzo*, and The Moor will surely supply you with whatever you need to explore all aspects of your creativity."

The young artisan spoke the truth. For, you see, unlike Venice and Florence, which were merchant republics, Milan had a ruling court. This would prove more conducive to my ambitions, both artistic and otherwise. It was a city-state ruled by a kind of dynasty, strongmen known as hereditary dukes. It had been run for decades by the Visconti family, and more recently, the Sforza, and Ludovico apparently felt the need to make his claim on power seem more legitimate. His court was full of creative artists, thinkers, charming ladies, engineers, problem-solvers, and military types. I suspected that the city could afford to spend handsomely on a mind such as mine. It would be an environment in which I could not only survive, but also thrive.

Maybe I would *start* as a planner of celebrations, I thought, but then I would make Ludovico grow to appreciate my many talents. He would promote me as a brilliant strategist for all things military. Then I would truly command respect. That would teach men like Lorenzo to underestimate me!

And besides, Milan had no evil priors trying to destroy me. Instead, it was a place where I could explore, live my life, and be happy.

I was not wrong, as time would tell.

Still, I could not help feeling personally insulted by the idea that I was to be relegated to the role of a mere court entertainer, as if I were nothing more than a silly jester or minstrel concerned only with ephemera.

Perhaps, as some pointed out, Lorenzo saw entertaining people as a truly worthy pursuit. He had been amusing Florence for years with pageants, passion plays, and all sorts of productions, especially in the annual pre-Lenten time of Carnival. I had worked on some of these.

Could this signal that he saw creating such shows as something to be proud of? Had he noticed my talents in this field, and decided to use them to his advantage with an important potential ally?

Of course, one thought that I have only recently entertained is the idea that, perhaps, just perhaps, Lorenzo saw something of my potential and had issued me an indirect challenge to prove everyone wrong by deliberately pretending to underestimate me. If this was Lorenzo's strategy for me, well then, I cannot deny that it has worked. Perhaps it was a stratagem cooked up by that clever Niccola Macchiavelli? I will never know…

Well, whatever the case, I decided at that time to take my chances and accept my fate. There were worse ones I could imagine than being sent to Milan.

Soon, I drew up a letter for the Regent of Milan, as Lorenzo instructed me to do. In those eleven paragraphs, I decided truly to "sell myself" to Ludovico Sforza, describing what I could do for him and his court. I wrote about my many talents and knowledge in areas such as architecture, engineering, directing waterways, and things with which I could improve and defend his city, including the weapons of war, such as bombards and the like, that I would be glad to design for him. At the end, I also added that, in peacetime, I would be able to create works for him, *"in scultura di marmore, di bronzo e di terra, similiter in picture,"* just so he would know that I could also create things of beauty, assuming he cared. Perhaps he *would* want me, I decided, and hopefully, it would be for things beyond an ability to plan silly parties and pageants.

Milano

Soon, as it turns out, Ludovico *did* want me, and I was on my way north, Atalante by my side.

I was given a sumptuous apartment in the *Castello Sforzesco*, and Atalante lived with me as my assistant (although everyone knew the real story). I was put to work, of course, as a planner of spectacles and plays to amuse the ducal court. Once my wounded pride had recovered, I learned that, much to my surprise, I rather enjoyed these jobs, as they appealed to my playful and theatrical nature. I admit that it was great fun to create dramatic tableaux for the court's amusement. Each was a problem to be solved, a piece of art and beauty to be savored, however ephemerally. It was an amusing and dynamic time, but I was disappointed not to be tasked with designing things to defend my new city, or to be able to improve its life through engineering projects.

Though he never said so, I believe, sadly, that The Moor never thought of me as much of a man, which is why he only gave me artistic things to do. However, he cared little about what I did on my own time, so long as I worked hard for him, so I cannot really complain. Also, I was given a few free hours most days in which I was able to pursue my various passions, especially mathematics and drawing.

LEONARDO'S LETTER

I took advantage of that stay in Milan to perfect my abilities as an observer and sketcher of people, even though I had little time for actual painting during my first years there. Just as I had done in Florence, I took up my folios and sketch pads, along with chalks and pencils, and found places to watch people in the various piazzas of my new Lombard home.

Milan was quite different from Florence, as I was soon to learn. The people were taller, more robust, and slightly lighter in hair color and complexion. Gentlemen oiled their hair in Lombardy, copying, I suspected, the style of Ludovico, *Il Moro*. I also noticed that they held themselves with greater confidence, perhaps due to the city's status as a fashion and financial center.

However, no one could rival, at least in my mind, the greatness of Florence. Wasn't our gold Florin the standard coinage used all over Europe? Whether one loved or hated the Medici, no one could argue with their success.

I noticed that, like in Florence, there was a large and burgeoning middle class, although it was not as numerous, or well-read, as in my home city. Like in Tuscany, the prosperous Lombard burghers were always elegantly dressed. They donned velvet doublets, felt hats, and the like. Those who could afford to do so boasted frocks of silk with bits of gold woven through them, and the women displayed beautiful bodices and ostentatious dresses. Even the feathers adorning the hats of nobles and wealthy merchants seemed exquisite. Soon, I traded my old clothes for a nice set of new velvet vests, silk tunics, and red hose of the finest quality.

It was in Milan where I especially began to study not only the bodies, but the physiognomy of those I observed, as faces reveal almost everything you need to know about people. I did everything I could to capture not only physical details of individuals from all walks of life, but also their emotions and feelings. I grew more and more fascinated by how various facial muscles contracted or changed to express a multitude of sentiments. Sometimes, I would follow men and women around all day, sketching them in a hidden folio, if I found their look compelling. I began to wonder: how did that lady use her upraised chin and slight smile, in conjunction with a fan and her lashes, to express flirtatious interest? How did that man clench his jaw just so, to show determination? How did we all use our muscles and tendons in concert to display, in a myriad of ways, what went on in our minds and souls?

This was when I began, Cecho, to pursue my obsession with human dissection in earnest. I used Atalante and his charms to find a priest who would allow me to sneak into an underground morgue, and I obtained a silver scalpel from a friendly surgeon. Soon, I began truly to know the human body inside and out, and to understand which muscles controlled which facial movements.

If only Andrea Verrocchio had known, years earlier, the turn my studies of human anatomy would take! Perhaps he would not have pushed me toward this macabre field of study had he suspected.

I am ashamed to admit this, but when *Il Moro* sent people to the gallows, I would make sure to be present with my sketchbook. At first, I told myself that I wasn't there to see criminals and enemies of Ludovico hang by their necks; I wanted to sketch the faces the people present would make, whether of disgust, excitement, or compassion. Of course, I also wanted to capture the men as they hanged, curious as I was about the human body in any position.

Of course, this fascination had begun back in Florence as a mere exercise to understand how the body functioned, to make me a better artist. However, Cecho, you know me well enough to understand how my mind works, and how one thing leads to another with my endless curiosity. Once I learned how one part of the human body performed, I had to keep going, hoping to understand it all. I yearned to unlock every mystery the human body held. Just as that boy discovering the mysteries of the hillside cave, my quest was to know everything I could, and how to connect science and art.

Of course, I do believe that, in addition to my learning about the human body, this obsession did *also* fulfill the original aim of making me a better artist, should anyone wish to complain.

Lady with an Ermine

I will never forget the day I first met Cecilia Gallerani.

It was in the autumn of 1489. Ludovico was deeply in love with her, even though she was barely sixteen, and had met her when she was but fourteen. Everyone referred to her as his *inamorata*. His love for her was not something the duke bothered to conceal, even though he was betrothed to another, my friend, Beatrice d'Este, the daughter of the Duke of Ferrara and sister of my dear friend, Isabella, the marquise of Mantua.

Ludovico called me into his private study, where he ordered me to suspend all my other projects, including a massive warhorse, to paint his beloved. She was carrying his child, he confessed, confirming the rumors that had made their way to my ears. He wanted me to paint her before the pregnancy became too obvious. So passionately in love was he that his most fervent desire was to preserve forever the youthful image of his lover. Such beauty, as everyone knows, is the most fleeting of things.

I set out to make the girl's acquaintance, having never had the pleasure of meeting her before. Ludovico's valet told me that I could find Cecilia taking a music lesson in Saint Ambrose's Basilica, as her family was a close friend of the priest who served there, a cleric who often gave her voice instruction. She liked to set her poetry, usually in Latin, to music for the delight of select audiences at court.

When I entered the Basilica, which I confess I had never done before, I was struck by how beautifully the light spilled onto the black and white of the floor through the windows of the apse at the far end. From there, a voice of angelic loveliness wafted toward me. I took my time walking toward it. I drifted forward, wanting to savor the moment, one that I sensed would be among the most delicious of my life. I glided along the nave as if in a trance, ignoring the gray colonnades, stained-glass windows, and other beauties of the place. The music drifted up to the ogive arches of that great place of worship. When I approached the altar, I could hear that the young woman had begun singing a version of *Ubi Caritas*, and I nearly began to weep. For it is true, Cecho, that wherever there is charity and love, God *is* there. And Cecilia inspired love and generosity of spirit in all those who knew her.

As I approached the front of the church, I first caught the eye of the aged priest, whose name was Father Piero. The white-haired old man stopped directing his pupil, his hand suspended in mid-air as he regarded me with surprise, his blue eyes wide and searching.

Just then, Cecilia snapped her head toward me with a look full of anticipation, rather than annoyance. What I saw was a face like no other. For a painter, the symmetry and beauty of this visage, those perfect, high cheeks framed by warm, auburn hair, which cascaded down onto a blue silk dress. She was like a divine gift. The look in her dark eyes conveyed a lively, playful curiosity and a thirst for experience and knowledge. This look told me that every interaction she had with unknown people was, for her, the opportunity to learn something new, a chance to be delighted.

If God had made me able to fall in love with any woman, I have no doubt I would have lost my heart to Cecilia that first time I laid eyes on her.

It was in that moment that I knew how I would depict her, something completely novel, a technique that would later be called *contrapposto*. I would paint her at an angle. Using all the expertise I had acquired of human anatomy as well as innovative techniques using the interplay of light and shadow, I would harness every skill I had to capture the remarkable spirit of this enchanting young woman. She would come alive through art, born anew with each viewing. I would preserve forever her spirit and image, just as I saw it at this very moment. With each gaze turned upon her, I told myself, one would notice something new.

This is what I set out to do, and this is what I accomplished, if I can once again speak of my skills without boasting overmuch. After all, it is not bragging if it is true, no? This portrait changed things, and the world of painting will never be the same.

The idea of the Ermine came to me later, and it was just the thing to draw the whole portrait together. A delightful pun on her name from the Greek word for the beast, *galli,* like her name, and, of course, the King of Naples had named Ludovico to the order of the Ermine the year before. But beyond these delicious puns for those in the know about such things, the ermine was, and continues to be, one of nature's most intriguing creatures, much like Cecilia herself. A symbol of moderation and purity, the white ermine eats only once per day, and would rather be caught by a hunter than sully itself by hiding in a dirty lair.

When at last I had her pose for me, I dressed her in a Spanish style. She wore a blue velvet open-armed gown with a square neckline edged with gold embroidery, a small cap, as well as a thin veil. The cap had a subtle, scalloped edge, which graced her forehead like a crown.

I drew her brown hair down under her chin and tied it there gently, almost with the tenderness of a father. Her hair was straight and parted down the center, as was the style then, wrapped in light silk.

Around her neck, I carefully arranged a string of onyx beads. I did my best to arrange these tastefully across her breast. I took my time to get everything just right.

I gave Cecilia a kitten to hold instead of an ermine. The tiny beast was so charmed by her that she was able to get it somehow to pose the way I asked. Once, when I had her turn to face me, posing her shoulders and arms just so, letting the light from the window fall at a forty-degree angle, I had Ludovico enter the parlor on cue, so that both girl and kitten turned to see him. At that moment, I sketched quickly to capture the image I wanted to portray. It pained me to have to ask her to return to this pose for several weeks afterwards as I worked, but Cecilia, besides being charming and lovely in every way, was also gracious and generous with her time, revealing a maturity far beyond her years.

The light from the ermine, as I pictured it, jumped gently from among the shadows and played on her face. The emotions reflected on her visage, in turn, were reflected onto the little beast, creating a narrative, a moving, almost swirling and spiraling piece that seemed to leap off the canvas.

I confess that a swell of pride rose in me as I saw, in my mind's eye, the painting come to life.

Just like with my Lisa many years later, Cecilia's smile was dynamic and ever-changing, depending on how one looked at the painting and even where one stood.

Something that almost no one knows is that I invited Atalante to join us during the most difficult days of this project. He would play his lute, which seemed to elicit a small smile from Cecilia, and, I like to imagine, made painting the ever-changing expression on her face easier to draw out thanks to the music that my student brought forth as an offering to her. In fact, when he tired of playing, sometimes he would recite Cecilia's own poems back to her. He had taken great pains to memorize them, which delighted her even further. He even improvised a playful Milanese accent that charmed us both.

LEONARDO'S LETTER

She rarely spoke to me during all of this, and she didn't have to. In life, as during the making of her portrait, as a court poet said of her, she seemed to listen, but hardly to speak. But when she *did* engage in conversation, she posed questions that revealed her great curiosity. One day in particular stands out in my memory, as she became quite verbose.

"Are there many men like you and Atalante?" she wanted to know.

I tensed when she asked me this, as men such as I never know how to talk openly about such things. However, when I replied cautiously that I estimated us at around one man in ten, she seemed to note the information and put it in the same category as when I had told her about my being left-handed.

"And how long did it take you to learn how to paint?" she inquired. I told her a bit about my youth with Verrocchio in Florence, and the process of learning the techniques of my art.

"Can you compose sonnets or other kinds of poetry?" she asked.

I admitted that, while I had studied the likes of Petrarch, Bocaccio, and Dante, I had focused on other arts than the written word.

"Can you and your ward play any other instruments besides the lyre and the lute?"

I chuckled and gently reminded her that, if she kept distracting me with so many questions, she would likely give birth before the painting was ever completed.

In any case, I was quite proud of my painting of the *Lady with an Ermine,* and Ludovico, Cecilia, and everyone else at court was as well. It remains one of my favorite works.

LEONARDO'S LETTER

Salaì

Soon, my life was about to change forever thanks to a devilish young man who would be by my side for decades.

Atalante and I parted ways on friendly terms, and I found myself suddenly alone. However, as so many have said, when God draws one chapter of our lives to a close, sometimes a new one is just about to begin. This was true when my lover left and I met Salaì, who would become my helper and assistant for many years.

I had just gotten up that day and was studying some sketches in my room. I had not begun to plan for the next court pageant yet, but knew that much work lay ahead of me, and I did not relish it. I had moved into one of the spare rooms given to me in the Sforza Palace and even took some of my meals with the other courtiers.

There came a knock at my door, and I turned to see a man dressed as a laborer standing by the open frame. He wore rough brown breeches and a humble peasant smock. He had removed a brown cap, which he gripped nervously before him. He couldn't have looked more out of place at the ducal court. I felt an irrational fear upon seeing this man, as I had had a nightmare of The Prior pursuing me the night before, so it was with a sense of disquiet that I greeted a stranger showing up unannounced.

Luckily, I had nothing to fear from this poor fellow. He strode into my room and looked down deferentially. Once he had done so, I saw a boy of perhaps ten standing behind him. The lad looked up at me, a sly smile crawling across his face.

"Master Leonardo, I presume," the man said. I nodded in agreement. "My name is Pietro di Giovanni. You wouldn't recognize me, but I work on the vineyard the duke has gifted you at Porta Vercellina."

A flash of embarrassment came over me that must have shown on my face. I had only been to that vineyard once or twice, and I did not recognize the man.

"Oh, I wouldn't expect you to recognize me," the man rushed to say. "I am but a tenant laborer."

"All right," I said. "Won't you please sit down? I apologize about the mess," I said, picking up a pile of drawings from a stool beside my desk, and inviting the boy, who I assumed to be his son, also to make himself at home.

"There's no need for us to sit," the man said with a nervous laugh. "I'd like to propose something to you," he said. I must have looked surprised, as he studied me as if I should have known what he was talking about.

The man looked down, still clutching his hat, and looked uncomfortable. He glanced at his son, who studied me openly with big brown eyes. I was almost surprised by the lad's insolence, but that was our Salaì.

"Go on," I said to the man. "Please feel free to say whatever you need to,*"* I said. I thought perhaps that he hoped to ask me about the vineyard, something I had not thought much about.

"This is my son, Giacamo," he said, nodding at the boy. "I will be honest with you. His mother and I can't do much with him. He can be…unruly, and we punish him often. But he says that he wants to come to court, to be an artist. I don't know if he has any talent," he continued after an awkward pause, "but someone told me you have no children, and could perhaps use an assistant," he continued. "Perhaps…perhaps we could entrust our boy to you for a time, and maybe he could live here and be your helper, and perhaps *you*, in turn, could teach him how to paint."

I could not have been more surprised if one of my flying machines had leapt off the page and taken flight right there before my eyes!

The truth was that I enjoyed my freedom, my independence, and the lack of children had left me plenty of time to pursue my many interests. However, it was also true that, since Atalante had left, I was somewhat lonely, unfocused, and more disorganized than usual. I suspected that I could do with some help, even if it was just a boy to run errands for me or do some tidying up (which, ironically, Salaì hardly ever did).

I looked at the lad, waved him to come closer. "Is that what you would like, Giacamo?" I asked, tousling his hair. "Would you like to come and work for me?"

The boy smiled at me and nodded as if he'd never wanted anything so much in his life.

I ran my hand over my beard and looked away. "Let me think it over," I said. "I will come to the vineyard soon to visit you and speak further about this," I said.

"Thank you, sir," the man said. "Let's go, Giacamo, and let Master Leonardo think."

Of course, dear Cecho, you will know that this is when Salaì became all but my officially adopted son. He helped me, it was true, and kept me company, but he was a liar, a thief, and a bothersome little devil, which is where his nickname came from.

Of course, he saved my life one day, and for that, I will be forever grateful. More on that another time.

Later, Salaì would join me at Santa Maria Delle Grazie. When dining with the monks there, I would often stare up at the walls of that great dining hall, envisioning how my fresco would grace that place and, I hoped, last for many, many years. My heart was to break upon learning how easily the painting would so soon begin to flake and deteriorate, but that is a passage for another day.

Madre Mia

Of course, as time went on, I advanced further in my work on *The Last Supper*. It was an all-consuming project that I threw myself into completely. I was determined to make it my magnum opus, the thing that defined my life and legacy as an artist. Every skill and bit of knowledge that I had accumulated in my decades of learning and exploring would make this mural something that would transform the world of art and shift how people thought of their relationship with each other and with God.

I had thrown myself so entirely into this work that I often slept all day and worked all night. So you can imagine my surprise when, one day in the late morning, one of the monks knocked on the door of my room to tell me that I had a visitor, and that it was a woman.

"She looks like a woman…of the life," the monk said, a whiff of disapproval in his voice. *"Una donna della vita."* I knew what this euphemism meant. Why would such a woman, one who had resorted to selling herself to survive, come to see *me*?

Upon opening the side gate of *Santa Maria delle Grazie,* the one usually reserved for beggars, laundresses, and cooks, I saw a downcast female figure who looked completely unknown to me. How, I wondered, could this person be looking for me? What could she possibly want?

When, at last, she pulled her blue hood all the way back, she revealed a mostly gray head and face that had once been beautiful, but now looked almost like that of a haggard old crone. I studied her countenance and sad brown eyes, and a flood of recognition washed over me.

It had been so many years since I had thought of her, much less seen her.

It was Caterina. My mother.

"*Mi dispiace, figlio,* I am so sorry, my son, I had nowhere else to turn," she began tearily, and I ushered her in.

She stood in the deserted refectory, the smell of bean soup wafting in from the kitchen, as she told me her story.

My stepfather, Antonio, had died a few years before, unsurprisingly in a brawl in a tavern. Her children, my half-siblings, had been unable to take her in, poverty-stricken as they were. My father's family had long ago stopped having anything to do with them. She had made her way to the city and appealed directly to my father, then still living a comfortable life in Florence. He had slammed the door in her face, probably ashamed for anyone to associate him with such a woman, even though she was someone with whom he had once produced a child. In desperation, she had turned to selling her body late at night in the Santa Croce neighborhood. As you can imagine, it was not easy for a woman of such advanced age to survive in such a way. I imagine that she was able to feed herself only by serving the absolute dregs of male society. I hate to imagine her debasing herself that way, all for a few measly coins men would toss her way after taking what little dignity she had left.

Predictably, she had ended up contracting a disease from a sailor, the one we Florentines like to call "the French curse," and had spent months suffering while being tended to by the brothers at Santa Maria Novella hospital. There was no cure for what she had, and she knew she would end her days in abject misery.

That was when a monk whispered to her one morning, as she sipped from a wooden cup that he held to her lips, that her son, the famous Leonardo, about whom she had been ranting in her sleep, was a well-off man in the court of the Duke of Milan.

Perhaps he had wanted to be rid of her, or just needed the bed for someone else. Maybe he was attempting to do her a kindness. In any case, Caterina soon packed her meager possessions into a travel bag and used her last bit of money to hire a carriage to convey her to Milan, in a last, desperate hope that her long-lost son, the artist from Vinci, would take her in. Without a doubt, the monk had suggested, her successful son could come up with some money to find some miracle cure for what ailed her.

I sighed when I heard this. Of course, I knew nothing of such cures. I refused to listen to the hoard of quacks and charlatans who plagued the Sforza court. However, basic shelter *was* something I could provide. And how could I refuse my own mother, however imperfect she was?

Sure enough, I rented a room at a nearby tavern and kept my parent there, in safety and relative comfort, for the remaining months of her life. I sent Salai to see her and care for her each day, and I visited her every chance I could pull myself away from my work.

Just as she had done with me when I was a child, I told her stories to entertain her. While she had told me about giants and flying creatures, I told her about the many adventures I had read of Marco Polo. I told her of my friend Rodrigo, how he had been the first to spot land on Columbus's voyage, and how they should name the new lands discovered there after him. I made up jokes and riddles to amuse her, and a smile sometimes crept onto her lips when I kept her company beside the dying evening fire.

"You always were a good boy, Leo," she said to me one night, reaching a fragile hand toward me. "So clever, so lovely, so caring. I know you must not be proud of me, but I am proud of *you,* my son."

I took her hand in mine and held it for a long time. I did not wish to lie and tell her that I was proud of her, but I was glad that she had come to see me, and I told her so. I think that this warmed her heart. I am glad that her last few months were spent in dignity and relative comfort.

LEONARDO'S LETTER

One night, as she lay resting, her chest gently rising and falling, I studied her for a long time, trying to remember her every feature. I felt that it would have been wrong to sketch her, but I wanted to remember her, and imprint her in my memory.

My mind wandered back to my childhood. I remember one day, when I was perhaps four or five years old. We were walking through the village square of Anchiano, a basket of laundry balanced on her head. I remember hearing the catcalls of the townsmen as her hand gripped mine. Unlike other women, who modestly ignored the calls of those bawdy fellows, I remembered my mother turning her head and glancing languidly at them, a half smile on her face. She seemed to relish the attention as they called out to her, "*Bellisima! Bellisima!*" as she was easily the most beautiful woman in that town.

I sighed. The memory was as fresh in my mind as if the scene had played out just days before. Only yesterday, my mother had been a woman of stunning beauty. And now, here she lay, wasting away before my very eyes.

How long before my own beauty would begin to fade? I glanced over at a looking glass. Despite my best efforts at concealment, a few lines had crept in beside my lovely eyes, and a few silver wisps of gray had found their way into my beard.

Tempis fugit, I whispered to myself in Latin. How time flies. Beauty, like all things, is fleeting. However, as the old saying went, *"ars longa, vita brevis."* Life may be short, but art lasts forever. Or at least, that is what I hoped.

I decided that I wanted to immortalize my mother in art. But how? I imagined a painting featuring her as a beautiful, radiant young woman, the way I remembered her, perhaps accompanied with a skull or some other *momento mori*.

Anyone who looked at her as she lay dying would see only a fallen woman. I, however, saw her as she once had been, a great and proud beauty, a person full of passion and love of life. To me, she was anything but a Magdalene; she was every woman all in one, Mother Mary, Mary Magdalene, and all women in between. She was beautiful and unique and special, but also, somehow, universal.

Not long after, in late June of 1495, Caterina died comfortably in her sleep. I paid for a tasteful funeral and for a mass to be said in her honor at Santa Maria Delle Grazie. I kept watch over her funeral bier for several nights, surrounded by torches and candles, and prayed for her soul, as a good and dutiful son should.

Once this was done, I was sad, but returned to the task at hand, and once again threw myself into my work with both gusto and renewed determination.

However, I had been inspired by a new idea.

Verrocchio had often told me in my youth about the popular practice of using a beautiful or effeminate youth to depict Saint John, Jesus's favorite disciple. "Saint John is the perfect depiction of men such as us!" Andrea cried one day as I modeled for him and some other artists. "He embodies the best traits of both men *and* women! It is through figures like John the Baptist and Saint Sebastian that men who love men can best express the passion of our faith." And so, a lifelong love affair had begun between me and that saint. As you know, Cecho, I recently finished a delightful painting of Saint John on sumptuous walnut.

I had begun painting the man sitting at the right hand of Jesus as a self-portrait. But now, I modified the cartoon to pay homage to the woman who had just passed from this world. I drew from my memories of Caterina as a young beauty.

I needed to draw viewers in so that they would see my masterpiece, did I not? And what better way to do so than with beauty.

Yes, the image of Our Savior's favorite apostle would still be partially a self-portrait. But, by feminizing some of John's features, it would also be a secret homage to my mother.

La Serenissima

Of course, all good things must come to an end, and my idyll at Milan was no exception. I shall have to come back to this time in another *récit,* if, for no other reason, to write more in detail about the time I spent painting *The Last Supper*.

For now, however, I shall write of my time in the most serene Republic of Venice.

First, let me remind you that King Louis decided finally to invade Milan in the fall of 1499. Salaì and I had been expecting this for years, so the attack was no great surprise. When it began, I was showing off my *Last Supper* to some art students, and I was trying to decide which ones to try to bed, when Salaì burst in with the news.

"Master!" he cried. "The French are coming. We must flee! *Subito, maestro*, right away!"

As usual, the young man was panicking and creating more drama than necessary.

As it turns out, it would be several weeks before we truly needed to take to our heels. Despite all the war planning I had done for Ludovico, he had put very few of my ideas into practice, so a Milanese defeat was imminent. This is sad, because, if he *had* taken those suggestions, it is my belief that we might have repelled the French invaders, and, for example, my giant equestrian statue might finally have been completed. However, to add insult to injury, the bronze I had requested for the actual finishing of the statue had been sent to make cannons, which were not even used correctly.

If only people would listen to me, especially when it comes to matters of warfare. But alas, in their eyes, I've always been no more than a silly *finocchio*.

The city was overrun in short order, and the French soldiers made great sport by using my marvelous clay model for target practice, firing arrow after arrow at my great creation in the piazza before the Sforza Castle.

So many years of study and work, and for what?

I at least wanted to protect the vineyard that Ludovico had granted me, and my assistant wanted to protect his aging parents who still worked there. As one of the men most visibly associated with the ducal court, I assumed, correctly as it happened, that my vineyard, and all my possessions, would be confiscated with no regard to my personal dignity. Luckily, I hid packets of money in my studio that they were unable to find, and I was able to recover years later.

My first stop as I went into exile from Lombardy was, as I have said, Mantua, where I hoped to make my home. The charming Isabella d'Este was, of course, the *marquesa* of that city-state, and although her husband

Francesco Gonzaga ran its military defense, the court was entirely the purview of this dear woman, one of the finest minds of Italy. Like Cecilia, whom I also found safe and sound in her court, I found my friend surrounded by a collection of books in various languages, as well as paintings, mostly by Montegna, her favorite — as can be expected, as she had been wholly impressed by my previous work, especially the portrait of Cecilia.

As you know, Isabella spent days both equivocating about whether I could stay, and then entreating me, over lavish dinners, to paint her. Sadly, I could guess that she never wanted to host me, as I could be a liability if the French invaded her little kingdom, and I had no desire to paint her in boring profile, as she insisted.

It was beyond me why such a lively and curious woman could suffer the thought of being painted in such a dull fashion after seeing *Lady with an Ermine,* but who can explain why one person likes one style of art and not another? In any case, I did make an impressive sketch of her, in profile, as she insisted, and took another copy with me, promising to make an oil painting of this, which I never did, busy as I was with other tasks. After all, there is more to life than money, and life is short, is it not? Far too short, no doubt, to spend it painting dull portraits, no matter how compelling the subjects may be. She could keep her Montegna, I thought ruefully.

In any case, I was able to gather my things, as well as a full purse and a letter of introduction from Isabella for the doge of Venice. Soon, Salaì, my other servant Zoroastro, and I joined a small band of desperate refugees from Milan who had the same idea. We soon found ourselves in a small cortege of carriages heading east to that most serene of cities, *La Serenissima,* the ancient Republic of Venice, where I hoped, for a time, to make my home.

Of course, our timing could hardly have been worse. Our Italian Peninsula was, indeed, besieged on all sides. Only that year, war had broken out between Venice and the Ottomans, and so the city where I had hoped to spend years of my life was anything but serene.

Of course, my reputation had preceded me, and Isabella's letter helped with the doge. Verrocchio and others, years before, had made many contacts with men like us in the governmental apparatus that helped me establish myself as a valuable artist and engineer. Before I knew it, Salaì, Zoroastro, and I were set up with a spacious floor of a divine palazzo rented from a Senator who held properties overlooking the Grand Canal. I could not have been more pleased with the situation. Hardly had we settled in before Salaì and Zoroastro donned blue capes and masks and began carousing through the streets with their new friends, singing bawdy songs and trying to, as Zoroastro said, "lift the spirits of the navy," who had suffered a crushing defeat just a few months before at the battle of Cape Zonchio. This was no laughing matter, I told my men, as the Ottomans could attack and overrun the canaled city at any time, but this did not stop Salaì from dressing in his finest silks and doublet, and Zoroastro from donning the rags of a harlequin with actors from a *Commedia dell'Arte* as they explored every bridge and courtyard near the Rialto. It was too frosty by then for them to plunge into the canals or try their hands at piloting one of the city's many elongated *gondolas,* but they found plenty of trouble to get into, even as November stretched into December.

Venice was, unlike Florence or even Milan, a truly established and regal city, confident and sure of her place in the world and her role in history, part of which led to her frustrating arrogance. She was a city of theatrics and illusion, commerce, fun, and cruelty, all in seemingly equal measure. Her business acumen and tradition of diplomacy had helped establish her as a uniquely strong republic. Like Athens before her, to which Venetians loved to compare themselves, *La Serenissima* saw herself as the most civilized city on earth, and, to my dismay, failed even to consider Florence. She even saw herself as protected by the Mother of God herself, and people told me at least once a day that *Madre Maria* would protect the city, thanks to her great virtue. Of course, Venetians seemed to think nothing of using prisoners of their wars as slaves or prostitutes (the city boasted of at least twenty *bordellos*, or so I heard), and the place was so full of an air of sensual pleasure and licentiousness that my two ruffians did not hesitate to enjoy themselves to the fullest.

It must be said that there was no carousing for *me* in Venice. I had been hired by the senate to help the Venetians devise plans for their defense against the Turks, a task I threw myself into completely. I spent long hours inventing ways that the *Serenissima* could defend herself against what I was sure would be an attack from the Isonzo River. The situation was dire, at least to my eyes, after Captain Grimani's defeat, and the weakening of her trade routes along the lands leading to the Levant.

Once again, alas, my expertise and hard work were to be ignored.

I still have some of the sketches and ideas among my old papers, none of which were put into practice. Couldn't a boat be submerged under the water, to spy, or perhaps attack the enemy? How about a suit with a space of glass with which to see underwater? Could a man with such a garment dive down with a long, snake-like apparatus leading to a floating package on the surface? With such a thing, several men could be hidden under the water as a stealthy fleet approached, and those very same men could then emerge from the water and commandeer a ship at the changing of the guard.

I will never forget the sting of humiliation as the old doge, Agostino Barbarigo, then almost eighty years of age, simply laughed at my plans as I presented them during the Christmas feast. I had a few defenders among the senators who had elected him, it is true, but almost none would speak out or defend my ideas, even when I showed how they could work. One of the ambassadors who had come with me from Milan, Dorini, tried to explain how brilliant I was, and that, if Ludovico *Il Moro* had only listened to my advice, perhaps things may have turned out differently in Milan. But the old leader just waved this away, taking a drink from his goblet and snorting his disapproval.

"These ideas are completely impractical," he said, taking a bite of ham. "How could a ship ever travel underwater? And a man be able to float on a ring, going upwards and down? Ridiculous!"

"I understand your confusion, excellency," said Senator Cavenaghi, the man in whose palazzo we were staying. "But what about the idea of the series of bulwarks that Master Leonardo has proposed? The man is gifted at geometry, and if he's correct, then the Ottoman galleys would never be able to penetrate our harbor. Maybe not even the outer islands."

The *Serenissimo Principe*, as the doge was sometimes called, seemed to contemplate this for a minute. "I don't know," he finally said. "Kemal Reis is a crafty man, and Constantinople has its share of engineers. Don't you think he could outsmart such a maneuver?"

"Perhaps," I responded. "But don't you think it's worth trying? What have you got to lose?"

The old man tented his fingers, seeming to contemplate what I had just said. His *cono ducale,* a horn-like bonnet covered in gold flecks and gems, which the leaders of this republic always wore in public, slipped down a bit on his forehead. The man stroked his long white beard as he appeared to try to decide what to say next.

"I expect we shall proceed with the plans as they've already been made," he finally said. "In the spring, we can have our mercenaries, and what's left of the navy, regroup in Cyprus. They will launch an attack from there on the Ottomans. Constantinople will be awash in the blood of the infidel!" he crowed.

"But, Excellency—"

"Our Republic has stood for almost a thousand years," the old doge continued. "I doubt a silly Ottoman Mamalook and his tiny fleet can destroy all that we've built, just like that!"

I sat back in my chair, trying not to let my frustration show. My eye fell on one of the diplomats from Ferrara across from me, and I tried to distract myself by memorizing the intricacies of the gold brocade of his diplomatic livery.

Ah, Venice. How frustratingly delightful the city was. Even the strange uniforms people wore to dinner could fascinate one.

It is true that I found this unusual city enchanting, like none I had seen before, but I began to wonder why they had hired me at all, if they refused to listen to my suggestions. After all, this was for the preservation of everything they held dear and had worked for centuries to create. Why did they refuse to examine every option?

A thought came to me then, which chilled my blood. What if The Prior had written to the doge, or some religious authorities, telling him to disregard whatever I suggested?

I stared at the doge, anger rising in me. Was a silly *finocchio* all I would ever be to these people, no matter how hard I worked or studied? Was I *never* to be taken seriously?

The old man did not seem to notice my anger or frustration. To tell the truth, I suspect he had already forgotten me.

"Come now," the doge said, clapping his hands. "Let's not look so glum. Bring out the minstrels!"

I only half watched the performance of the minstrels and troubadours. I tried to enjoy the show. It was a troop from Verona, and they accompanied their songs with oversized lutes and performed acrobatics, with one of them even spitting fire. Finally, one of them told a story about a young couple who had fallen in love though they were from opposing families, but before they got to the end, I got up and walked out of the Ducal Palace.

Soon, I found myself standing alone in the *Piazza San Marco*. I studied the elaborate structure of the *campanile,* or belltower, next to the Ducal Palace, and walked over to the little porch at its base, designed by the architect Sansovino. This little place was known as the *loggetto.* It had been inspired by ancient Rome, and contained several bas-reliefs and statues, representing various supposed "virtues of the Republic," for Venice to emulate. The city herself was personified as Justice, wielding a sword and lording over two lions. Minerva stood for wisdom, such as the wisdom of the Venetian democracy, which they saw as a modern manifestation of Roman ideals. Statues of Apollo, Venus, the goddess of love and beauty, and Mercury, the god of commerce and eloquence, all spoke volumes about how *La Serenissima* saw herself. The final statue was an allegory of peace, the ultimate virtue. It all reminded me of the paintings that Sandro had done for the Medici. I sighed deeply. If only I had witnessed wisdom and a desire to defend commerce, peace, and justice on the part of the Venetians.

Beauty was everywhere here, but for how long? I felt as lonely as Apollo just then. He was the god of the sun, *il sole,* I mused, which seemed so close to the word *solo,* which is exactly how I felt as I stood alone there, contemplating these symbols of the city.

Soon afterward, I drifted across the piazza, and stood for a while staring up at the great Cathedral dedicated to Saint Mark, which I had been too busy to study up until then. So close was this city to the Turks that I noticed a clear Byzantine influence in the façade of the great edifice, then illuminated by torches and the soft light of the moon. I resolved to explore the structure when I found time enough to do so.

Part of me wanted to walk over to the Rialto Bridge, near my lodgings, but instead I walked down to the water, just behind the Palazzo Ducale. I turned left, and found myself meandering along the water's edge, across bridges and through narrow streets and alleyways touching the *Canale di San Marco*. Before long, I realized that my feet had led me to the *Campo Santi Giovanni e Paolo,* in the Castello quarter. I looked up, and there before me, to my delight and sadness, was the equestrian statue of Bartolomeo Colleoni, completed by my master and friend, Andrea Verrocchio, who had passed on by then.

I thought of the great horse I had tried to build in Milan.

I studied the intricate work of the bronze statue. Somehow, it balanced on three legs, perched majestically upon a pedestal, with one hoof raised as if charging into battle. The strength conveyed by this military man's figure was impressive. My old friend had worked on this for eight years, and I imagined that this piece would stand for centuries, allowing both Verrocchio and Colleoni to be immortalized through art for all the ages.

What did *I* have to show for my work? A few paintings of beautiful people, a doomed *Last Supper* whose paint was flaking off a little every day, a folio of ideas for things that would never be made. My ephemeral work on pageants in the court at Milan, which had surely been forgotten, or soon would be.

Would no one take seriously the work of Leonardo from Vinci?

LEONARDO'S LETTER

I had always fought against feelings of melancholy and self-pity, seeing these as useless, wasted emotions. But now, standing before this great creation of Verrocchio, my late mentor and friend, I could no longer control how I felt.

I sank down onto the stones of that square, buried my face in my hands, and cried, as a light snow began to fall.

After a little while, I pulled myself together and walked over to one of the nearby low bridges, the kind that are everywhere in Venice.

I looked down into the water below me. The dark canal was illuminated by moonlight, and I stared into my reflection.

Who was I? What was I doing?

*

Two months later, while charmed by the city on the canals, I had to admit defeat. I still hadn't gotten anywhere with my military plans. I was unable to convince the stubborn Venetians to carry out much of anything. I will admit, however, that I enjoyed the chance to sit and write and reflect, and I could not complain about our lodgings. Many days, even though it was winter, I worked at a desk that gave onto the canal, and I fully enjoyed the view. I had to admit that the city was full of enchantment and a special light like nowhere else. I grew to understand the local *Veneto* dialect, which was much harder to master than

Milanese. I also grew to appreciate the local culture and explore St. Mark's Cathedral, among other places of worship.

I learned that the Venetians were a proud people, an innovative and enterprising lot who had a vast commercial and diplomatic network stretching far and wide. Not only did they trade with Constantinople, or had before the war, but their empire reached all the way to Sardegna and Lepanto, and they had agents in faraway places, such as Barcelona, Paris, even London. Their republic had lasted over six centuries, and I was impressed at the strength and history of their institutions. Even though it was the wealthy and powerful that comprised the senate, who in turn elected the doge, who reigned for life, there was a sense of pride at being Venetian by men of all walks of life, from the lowliest gondolier and baker to their leader himself. I could see why Salaì never wanted to leave, and why Zoroastro, who also enjoyed women and had been bedding a young widow for weeks, had resolved never to leave.

"Master Leonardo," he said, "you've got to stay at least until the annual regatta. We will leave from Santa Maria della Salute, and then we'll round the islands and be back before you know it. It will be sometime in the spring, and my team of rowers will surely win!" he said with the confidence of youth.

"I doubt that we will stay that long," I said, patting him on the arm. "Salaì and I need to get back to Florence, where I will start my life over again."

"But you *must* stay!" the young man insisted, his blue eyes showing great disappointment.

"I'm afraid not," I said. "Salaì should be glad that I've given in and allowed him to stay through *Carnivale*."

And, indeed, even though I had wanted to leave with the new year of 1500, once it became apparent that I would get nowhere with the old doge, Salaì had thrown a tantrum, and I had given in. The tales of Venice's pre-Lenten celebrations were legendary, and I confess that I, too, wanted to see them before heading back to Florence at long last. Salaì was right, after all — after nearly eighteen years away, what difference did a few more weeks make?

I must admit that it was worth the wait. What a scene it was! *La Serenissima* was full of merriment, hordes of drunken young men dressed as jesters, maidens with flowers and ribbons in their hair, and groups of raucous young people playing flutes and beating drums. It was impossible to feel glum in such a celebration.

Salaì and I attended a masked ball, and the music from the lutes and recorders was both whimsical and invigorating. I had not danced with a woman since jumping into a *chiarantana* country dance, adapted for the court, with Isabella years before in Milan. For this ball in Venice, I was paired with a lovely blonde beauty named Lucrezia, a distant cousin of the doge. The women of the ducal court suspected the kind of man I was, and therefore they often felt comfortable conversing with me and, during festivals such as these, placing their hands on mine and joining me in a friendly turn.

The following day, we joined the Venetians in watching the doge's procession, in which their elderly leader led a cortege from his palace through the piazza in front of Saint Mark's Church. The old man was bedecked in his yearly regalia, which consisted of his richly colored purple gown, gold-colored slippers, and the *cono ducale* crowning his head over a cap of red velvet and ermine trim. In his hand, he carried a gold scepter, and he was preceded by a group of all the city's parish priests and a group of boys dressed as acolytes. During this ceremony, the doge walked to the shore of the canal and threw a gold ring into the water, thus symbolizing the marriage of Venice to the sea.

Once this was over, I retired to my rooms and tried to get some sleep, having already packed my trunks earlier. However, a night of slumber was quite impossible. Bands of drunk young men, including, without a doubt, my two ruffians, carried on singing and calling out to each other all through the night. When at last Salaì appeared in the early afternoon of the following day, exhausted from too much wine and song, I knew that we would not venture forth that day, and I had to walk down to the pier, grumbling the entire way, to let my boatman know that I would require his services on the morrow, instead of at that time.

The things we do for love and friendship!

At least you, my dear Cecho have never given me such trouble.

LEONARDO'S LETTER

Volta a Firenze (Return to Florence)

Words cannot describe how happy I was to be back in Florence!

As can be expected, much had changed while I was away, even though her Tuscan beauty, while beaten and tarnished, still breathed under a weary and fearful surface.

I had followed the events as they unfolded in my home city from afar, mostly through visitors and emissaries from the Medici, but as I had been kept so busy by Milan court life, among other pursuits, I had not allowed myself to follow the story too closely.

When I left in late 1482, the reign of terror of Savonarola was only a distant threat on the horizon. Years later, by 1494, he had completely taken over the city. While the Medici had been mostly willing to look the other way as men such as I lived our lives the way we saw fit, the new extremist monk was the exact opposite. Soon, the love between men was a main target of the fanatic and, some would say, Savonarola's main obsession, so much so that wicked tongues whispered that he was a sodomite as well. No man hates that which he does not see a bit in himself, no?

Apparently, as the stories went, bands of handsome young men were enlisted to try to entice and entrap men like us into sinful acts, and then, when things began to happen, guards would be called to catch the offenders *in flagrante delicto.* Of course, many artists and free-spirited men were targets of this campaign, and the ranks of my friends and acquaintances were much thinner all these years later than the day I left. Even though I had not wished to leave for Milan, it is quite likely, as I look back now, that Lorenzo *il magnifico,* now dead, had saved my life instead of ruining it.

I thought back to the story of the weeds being separated from the wheat and burned in a furnace, and shuddered.

I did not dare to ask anyone if my old enemy, The Prior, was still alive. I reminded myself, however, that he was elderly when I departed in 1482. How could he possibly still be haunting the streets and alleyways so many years later?

When news of my homecoming spread among the artists in the quarter near *Il Duomo*, I knew it was only a matter of time before Verrocchio's Verrocchio former students and friends organized a banquet to welcome their old colleague home. Sure enough, no sooner than the day Salaì and I had settled into our spacious home near the Ponte Vecchio, a handsome young blond named Vincenzo was sent to invite us to Andrea's old workshop that very evening.

Far from the festive event it could have been, my "welcome home" dinner was a solemn affair, full of commiserating artists telling tales of torture and terror.

I tried not to look disappointed. I sympathized with what my friends had gone through, but was it so wrong of me to hope for some merriment upon my return?

"Maestro Leonardo," said one ruddy-faced artist named Luca, "you cannot know what it was like, living in such fear during those years." And he was right, of course. Except for that time when I was briefly arrested in 1476, I was largely untouched by such horrors, and even then, I had felt sure that the charges would go nowhere.

"So many of us were rounded up," the young man continued, his voice breaking a little. "So many dead, or in prison, some hanged or stoned, the lucky ones had their heads chopped off or were garroted before the flames could get to them."

I shuddered when I thought of death by fire, what the Spaniards, in their Inquisition, called "*quemadero*." I had, on occasion, momentarily held my hands over a flame to see what it felt like, and I remain convinced that this is, by far, the worst way of all to die. I feel lucky, my dear Cecho, that I shall soon pass away here in this comfortable bed, with you by my side. All men should be so lucky.

"Did you hear about the...*falò delle vanità*?" the young man asked.

I looked down at my cup of wine and frowned. I felt a mixture of relief and guilt that I had not been there to fight against the senseless burning of things of beauty, this "bonfire of the vanities," the likes of which had been carried out by religious zealots for nearly a century. The story of Florence's bonfire had become the stuff of legend; Savonarola had defied even the pope and ordered all manner of things collected into a massive mound before the *Duomo* back in February of 1497, on the day that should have been Shrove Tuesday. He must have chosen that day to send the message that, not only would any kind of amusement or pre-Lenten celebration *not* be allowed, but indeed, he would not tolerate anything that promoted the sin of *vanitas*. Therefore, all that he and his minions deemed dangerous was thrown onto the pyre, such as books, sheets of nonreligious music, art that depicted themes from the ancient world, even mirrors and women's makeup. All of these and more had been consigned to the flames.

I noticed that Botticelli had not said much during the dinner, but now he spoke. "I myself had to toss my beloved *Zeus and Ganymedes* into the fire," he said, and I could hear the heartbreak in my old lover's voice. "It was *il mio capolavoro*, my greatest work. I spent years on it, getting every detail just right."

This was before I had begun work on my portrait of Lisa. I briefly thought of what it might feel like to be forced to cast my fantastic portrait of Cecilia and her ermine into such a bonfire. I winced at the thought. I liked to think that I could never do such a thing, but when I considered the idea of the terror of the *quemadero*, I knew in my heart that I would burn a thousand paintings if I thought it would spare me such a torment.

A pall of silence fell over the dinner, during which, I imagine, each man present wondered whether life and health were worth sacrificing for art. What was art, after all, without life?

I reflected on Botticelli's predicament. I could imagine how much this painting meant to my friend; I had heard about it even in Milan. He had used two of his favorite models to pose as that duo who was, perhaps, the most iconic representation of *amore masculino* ever to exist. I could also only imagine how hard it had been for him to pretend to be devoted to the Dominican Friar, which he did so that he could save his skin and avoid the flames himself.

Since as long as anyone can remember, men like us have had to do whatever it takes to survive.

Luckily, the citizens of Florence overthrew Savonarola in 1498, but his devotees, known as *Piagnoni,* still kept the memory of their master alive, while trying to destroy anything with a whiff of humanism or paganism that they considered dangerous for the immortal souls of Tuscans. Still, these (mostly young) men were a small minority. The Medici remained out of power, but we all expected them to return to it soon enough. Indeed, as difficult as that family could be, they were reliable patrons of the arts who, like my friend the Duke of Milan, seemed not to care who slept with whom, so long as work on their behalf got done and the private lives of artists and thinkers remained at least somewhat private.

I had not yet seen The Prior since my return, and the fear of asking about him made me hold my tongue. Part of me hoped to learn of his death, but another, greater part of me feared he still stalked the streets. Maybe it was my imagination, but I felt his lurking presence in this city that I yet loved. My old enemy would be an ancient troll by then, but I still knew better than to underestimate him.

That night, someone whispered that he had been Savonarola's right-hand man, and still secretly pulled the strings of those young devotees who remained loyal to the fanatical monk's memory. What power or secrets could that old crow muster to keep those men in his thrall, if indeed it was him? I hoped the man who told me this was mistaken, or had perhaps confused The Prior with someone else, although I could think of no one as sinister as my old nemesis.

I closed my eyes, took a deep breath, and forced my ancient enemy from my mind. It was better, I decided, instead to think about what I would do now that I was back among friends and in my lovely home city. I still had decades ahead of me, God willing, and it was time to decide how to spend them.

"And what do you plan to do now, Master Leonardo?" asked an assistant to the late Andrea Verrocchio. "We have all heard of how brilliant you are in the world of architecture and mathematics. We even heard of your military planning and...a giant horse?" he continued, much to the amusement of everyone present. I was glad he did not bring up my *Last Supper*, as the thought of that masterpiece dying a slow death in Milan tortured me to no end. "To what will you devote your time now?" he asked with a wry smile. "Surely *not* to the study of cadavers."

Nervous laughter rippled through the gathered artists. I had done this much more in Milan, but of course had begun to explore that practice during my early years in Florence. My old friend and former pupil, Lorenzo di Credi, looked at me with recognition in his handsome brown eyes. He alone understood how important it was to me to study anatomy. For years in the time of our youth, before fleeing to Seville in Spain during the Savonarola reign of terror, he had accompanied me to the morgue and the homes of surgeons after dark as we flaunted the church's proscription of studying corpses.

I was, apparently, famous among these men for many things, some of which were good, and some, less than admirable.

However, I had made my decision, at least for now. I had had enough of engineering, architecture, mathematics, the art of war, and the like. I even felt no desire to put scalpel to flesh right then. No, mine would henceforth, and for the foreseeable future, be a more noble and pleasurable pursuit.

I would avenge the great injustice done to the likes of my dear Sandro and others during those harsh years. Yes, I would channel my genius into art and make them all pay for what they had done!

"Gentlemen," I declared, placing my goblet on the table in front of me and puffing out my chest, so much so that my doublet almost burst, "I shall now dedicate all my time and devotion to painting!"

Hypocrisy and Bohemia

Of course, like so many of my pronouncements, this promise I would break within the week.

The temptation to try other pursuits was too strong. Even though I have gained my fame mostly through art, I have never been able to forswear a myriad of other passions. Luckily, I have rarely been forced to choose; my circumstance of having been born a bastard of whom nothing is expected, and my being a man on whom Heaven chose not to bestow fatherhood, are twin blessings for which I thank God every day, free as I was and am to pursue whatever I wish.

Of course, it was also during this time that my bad habits of staying up late, sleeping most of the day away, being incredibly disorganized, and only working in spurts of frantic, creative energy became even worse.

Soon, I took it upon myself to rebel, as much as I could and in every way, against the kind of "Christian renewal" that Savonarola had called for.

This was the time when I was knocking on the door of my fiftieth year, or as Dante had so eloquently put it, *"Nel mezzo del cammin di nostra vita."* As if taken by a whim, *subito,* my dear Cecho, *subito*, I felt, for some reason, compelled to be, as we Tuscans love to say, un *cattivo terribile,* a playful kind of naughty man.

I cannot explain it, other than to say that I desired to flaunt who and what I was before the ghost of Savonarola, who had been hanged and burned in the center of Florence less than three years before. I wanted to show The Prior, if he were still alive, and his army of young men, those who went around with a permanent scowl on their faces, that *I* would not be cowed, that *I* would live my life happily the way that *I* wanted to, for the first time ever, following my own rules.

If important men, when looking at me, only saw a silly *finocchio,* well then, a *finocchio,* in all his unbridled glory, is what they would get!

I began to dress in an especially extravagant, flamboyant way. It is true; I drew unnecessary attention to myself, and so did Salaì. Every time I walked past the *Piagnoni,* I would stare at them, often directly in their eyes, provoking and daring them to do something. But their "great leader" was gone, so what could they do to me now? His army of spies were, after all, no more than a band of leaderless boys. The new ruler of Florence, Soderini, was probably just temporary, but this man was a pragmatic ruler who had nothing to do with the fanaticism of the Dominican monk. I had heard that Soderini had little patience for fanatics who wished to cause trouble and disrupt the proper functioning and commerce of his city.

And if The Prior, or someone like him, tried to come after me yet again, well, he would regret *that*, I decided. I was a successful gentleman artist, from an important and well-connected line of men, with friends in high places and nothing left to prove.

Men like me had truly made Florence what it was, the envy of Europe. My city had lost its way, yes, but I was going to help it find its way *back* to greatness and glory. We would outdo even Venice! And while I was at it, *perbacco*, I would show my fellow *finocchi* that it was safe to be ourselves once again.

I donned the most conspicuous outfits I could; I chose provocative purple and pink stockings, a rose-colored Catalan cape, a taffeta gown with velvet lining, a dark-purple satin coat, an Arab hood, and, when I was feeling quite outlandish, a burgundy cloak with a velvet capuchin. One day, I shelled out three whole ducats to Salaì — it is true, I could deny him nothing! — and he got himself similar rose- and pink-colored hose with a bejeweled cloak of silver with green trim.

I took on some commissions, and soon began a cartoon of what would later be a splendid painting of the Madonna and child, yet including, surprisingly, Saint Anne and Saint John. It was an ambitious work, but one that I knew I could do, and do well. I suspected it would be difficult, but it would be a satisfying and almost joyful process, or at least, one that would make me happy. Over and again, my mind returned to the equestrian statue that my late friend had wrought in Venice. This, *this* would be my greatest work, my legacy. *This* would help me to achieve what a sin-free life could not: immortality.

At least, that is what I *thought*. Until the day I saw *her* at the market, a day when I did not even intend to go and had considered sending Salaì instead.

I had just freed a dove from its cage when I looked up and saw her, the only woman I would ever truly love, even though she belonged to another — in this case, Francesco del Giocondo. There she stood before me, the hint of a mischievous smile on her lovely, luminous face.

Lisa Gherardini del Giocondo.

*

But my greatest work, the one that, unlike my *Last Supper,* will stand the test of time, my *capolavoro,* my lovely *Lisa,* which, thankfully, there was no Savonarola to burn, was to come later. For now, I would dedicate myself to one of my favorite works, for which I was hired by the good brothers of the Church of *Santissima Annunziata.* The Servite monks there had already asked my friend and probably distant cousin, Filippo Lippi, to create an altarpiece for their lovely church; however, when I made it known that I would be interested in the commission, the man kindly bowed out and let me have it. The fact that my father did all of their legal paperwork may have helped as well. In any case, the monks invited me and Salaì to move out of my newly rented space and into five guest rooms at *Santissima Annunziata*.

This monastery, attached to the church where I would paint my *Saint Anne*, was like heaven for me. Those years were among the happiest of my life, even if I had not yet met my dear Cecho (do not be cross, my love). I was happier there than anywhere before, even more than my tempestuous and hectic time in Milan.

Why, you might ask, was I so happy? Well, the monastery, besides being full of the company of men, some of whom would occasionally visit me in my rooms, also allowed me to create a space in which artists and artisans worked together in a way that would have made old Verrocchio proud. Furthermore, the place held the most amazing library I have ever seen before or since, and, as you know, I had become a converted bibliophile by then. It boasted no fewer than five thousand volumes, and I spent long hours there satisfying my every whim and curiosity, often reading late into the night. I can still remember the light of my candles flickering off the window panes, while wondering what made the fire behave the way it did, and how the little flame created a dancing, sprite-like reflection on the glass, rising, twirling, then falling playfully, not unlike the swirls and eddies I had observed in the stream as a child.

Then, Salaì would enter the room with my evening meal on nights when I did not join the brothers for their evening repast, and I would sup with my naughty pupil before getting down to work in the adjoining room that I had set aside for the altarpiece. Indeed, my usual bad habit of staying up late to work far into the early morning hours only grew worse during this time, and I would often sleep in until midafternoon. Luckily, the monks were only too kind with me, allowing me to do as I pleased. I imagine that they were just happy to see the work progress, as I know I have had, at times, the reputation of one who fails to complete every project as promised, or on time.

Speaking of unfinished projects, I must confess here one of the great regrets of my life; it is true that I never painted anything for Isabella d'Este, even though I had promised to do so. Maybe I should have, but I just could not bring myself to do it.

It was terribly *cattivo* of me.

Perhaps it was stubbornness, or maybe I resented her for not taking me in when I had come knocking in Mantua, but for whatever reason, I never did paint her portrait, and I still feel a bit guilty for a promise unkept.

Indeed, I will mention the poor Friar Pietro de Novellara, a good fellow whose time we wasted as he was stuck in the middle of this senseless battle of wills. The unfortunate man tried at first to cajole, then threaten me to complete the painting, for which I had created a sketch, you may remember, during my visit to Isabella's court.

I evaded this task for years, however, and never really intended to create that mediocre painting in profile, even though it would have fetched a high price; I could have lived without lifting another brush in my life, had I wanted to. I suppose the reason I always resisted, even when Isabella herself came to find me (I invented a trip to the countryside to study the flight of birds when she came), was that I knew my old friend well, well enough to know that she only cared about having a painting done by my hand to impress people; she appreciated nothing of true beauty, despite her impressive culture, refinement, and education. That said, she *was* a friend, a patroness of the arts, and I should have made time to do what I had promised, and for that, I am truly sorry. My uncle had always taught me to keep my word, after all.

Alas, the time to paint her is long past.

At least she had her works by Montegna.

But back to a description of that enchanting time of my life.

One of the things I loved most about my new situation was that on evenings when I was not working on my commission, I was able to visit the nearby Santa Maria Nuova hospital, or the one at Santo Spirito. Late at night, I would sometimes steal away and knock thrice on the door of the morgue, when the guard would let me in, once we were sure no one was watching. Florentines denied me nothing in those days. Sometimes, Lorenzo would come along, as Salaì had no desire in accompanying me on such macabre missions, and cared nothing about how the human body worked, beyond the male *cazzo*. Lorenzo and I would creep down the long, spiral staircase to where the deceased lay on cold stone slabs. We filled notebook after secret notebook, and my knowledge of what made the human body work grew ever more profound. I grew to suspect that, contrary to what some of the surgeons believed, the heart was that which pushed the blood through our veins, and that the preoccupation with bleeding, leeches, and a balance of the humors was all wrong. However, I kept these thoughts to myself, although perhaps I should have shared them.

But...I digress, and should return once again, to the topic of art.

It is true what they say of my famous altarpiece; I went back and forth, and then back again, on the composition of my *Saint Anne*. To be accurate, I should say what I mean. The painting I labored over for years was, more accurately, one in which Mary and her mother sat together, while an infant Jesus reached for, at first, his cousin, Saint John the Baptist. As anyone who knows me can tell, I am a devotee of Saint John, and I am quite proud of my painting of him pointing to heaven, which I just finally completed for my friend, King Francis, likely my final commission. However, the painting in question, *Virgin with Child and Saint Anne,* was to be the high altarpiece of the *Santissima Annnuziata.* As fate would have it, it never hung there, and I did not complete it for years.

At first, I wished to show Jesus interacting with Saint John, but some of the artists I consulted insisted that I show him wrestling a lamb, thus symbolizing the later

Passion. Of course, the monks each had a different opinion about what the painting should eventually look like and contain, although they were good enough to point out that they would be happy with *whatever* I painted, so long as I completed the job, and it contained Mary and her Holy Mother. This was their only real stipulation.

For the first time in many years, I was happy. I was living rent-free, living openly with Salaì, whom people assumed was my lover, and my life was joyful and easy. I enjoyed a level of professional success and public respect that I had never experienced before in my home city. Even my father's children, my half-siblings, often invited me to dinner, and introduced me, with pride in their voices, as "Uncle Leonardo." I even felt sure that I would soon conquer my dream of flight.

But like the ancient story of Icarus, I had flown too close to the sun on gossamer wings. It was time for me to come crashing back to the ground, as so often happened when I felt too proud, too free from torment, too full of myself.

As fortune or God would have it, that is when I saw him. Where else? At the market.

I remember the day as if it were this very morning. I was talking with a young notary who had worked for my father. We stood near the fountain in the *Piazza della Signoria*, where the market bustled before us, where Savonarola had been killed, and where the Bonfire of the Vanities had been held. I had just tucked a lace handkerchief into an elaborate purple sleeve when I looked up. My gaze was drawn to the left, where something told me that angry eyes were watching me.

And, as bad luck would have it, there he was, alive, against all odds and the laws of nature, contrary also to what I believe is the will of God.

The Prior.

Amazingly, he looked as if he had not aged a bit since the day I had left. The devil! How did he do it? Everyone I knew, including myself, had aged every one of those eighteen years. I had taken to boiling the husks of hazelnuts to try to perfect a dye that would keep my hair the same color it had been when I was young. Yet, there he stood, motionless, studying me like a hawk, or perhaps a buzzard, a vile old bird in any case, just crouching, waiting for me to make a mistake or grow weak so that he could attack with delight. His ancient face was still a disaster, his nose hooked, his ruined cheeks crossed and scratched with wrinkles. His jet-black eyes studied me under white eyebrows and a crown of colorless, tonsured hair.

I imagined he was a demon from Dante's Inferno come just to torment *me*, my own evil shadow as it were, and that, try as I might, I would always be unable to shake him.

He saw me, dressed in an outrageous pink doublet and hose of the same color, and his eyes showed recognition. He had not forgotten me. I could never be so lucky as to hope for that.

I turned as if to flee, and my young friend walked quickly away, as if he sensed that something evil was afoot. I wanted to escape, but the old man strode right up as I stood there, frozen, helpless beside the fountain that blocked my exit.

"So, the little bird has chosen to return to his Tuscan nest," The Prior said, his voice raspy, yet somehow, still compelling. Something from beyond the grave. If burned paper and flesh could have a sound, this would have been it.

"The return of the Prodigal Son," he murmured, almost slithering around me.

"Yes," I was able to mumble.

"Well, we are glad to have you back among us, *caro Leonardo*," he said. "You really ought to come see me for confession sometime," he said, his voice smooth, before hissing the name of the church of which Savonarola had put him in charge. "If you come, I will clear my afternoon for you," he whispered in my ear. I could barely believe what was happening. Was my old enemy trying to *seduce* me?

"I sense that your eye is still fine for the arts, *finocchio*," he said, his voice still low. "It would be such a shame if you were to burn for your sins, especially for those of pride and vanity. However, if you come to see me, perhaps I can—"

"No, thank you," I was able to mutter. "I see Father Giuseppe, in Santa Maria Novella," I added, feeling trapped in a waking nightmare.

He stared at me for a while, as if studying me, and his disastrous mouth twisted into what passed for a smile. "Welcome home, *carissimo*," he whispered before turning back to the market. "You haven't seen the last of me."

After he crept away, I sat down hard on the edge of the fountain and buried my head in my hands. My entire body shook.

How could he still be *alive*, and why was I still so afraid of him?

What I had told The Prior was only a half-truth. I had agreed to see the kindly priest when I had the time, but it had been years since my last confession. Perhaps this was a sign that I should go and talk to him.

I whispered to myself the verses from Lamentations that always brought me peace, especially when I worried that my sins had been too numerous:

"For no one is cast off from the Lord forever. Though He brings grief, He will show compassion, so great is His unfailing love. For He does not willingly bring affliction or grief to anyone."

I breathed in and out, slowly regaining my composure. I splashed water onto my face from the fountain. Slowly, after a little while, I felt better.

LEONARDO'S LETTER

I truly believed, and still do, that God would not willingly bring affliction or grief to anyone. Cecho, I still firmly believe that God is Love, universal and unconditional Love.

But, I wondered, why did our Holy Father seem to enjoy tormenting me, or at least testing me, with someone like The Prior? He was like my own personal cross to bear, my own *Via Crucis*.

STEVEN FARRINGTON

Contra Michelangelo

Many have wondered about my legendary rivalry, and disdain that truly was mutual, for that most annoying of Florentine upstarts, Michelangelo Buonarroti.

I had been back in Florence for about a year when I made the acquaintance of the young man I had spied as a boy all those years before working in the Medici sculpture gardens.

I will freely admit that, on the evening in question, I was being, as they say again, among the eccentric world of Tuscan artists, *un cattivo terribile.*

In my defense, though I admit that it is a weak one, it was during a sumptuous dinner at Botticelli's. I had almost held the gathering in my rooms at the *Santissima Annunziata*, but at the last moment decided that the sight of so many humanists who favored *amore masculino* might be too much for the brothers of the monastery to take, tolerant as they were of my eccentric ways. Their kindly prior had never hidden his conservative nature, even if he seemed perfectly willing to look the other way, so long as I held out the promise of a great altarpiece for their church.

The week before, I had thrown a well-attended party to which the cream of Florentine society came to marvel at my cartoon showing a youthful Saint Anne and Mary holding Baby Jesus reaching out to his cousin, a cherubic Saint John. Soderini and his entourage, as well as representatives of the Borgias, had all seemed impressed, the wine had flowed, and art students sketched what was already deemed by most a splendid masterpiece. The long-suffering head of the monastery had looked satisfied during the entire evening, wrongly convinced as he was that a completed painting would soon grace a place of prominence in his church.

However, when Botticelli offered to host this dinner, I accepted, not wanting to push my luck too much with my hosts.

So, back to my being *cattivo*.

When I saw the young sculptor, seated across from me at Sandro's large table, I felt a strange desire to try to impress him. It is true, my dear Cecho; sometimes, when the wine flows freely, and when I spy handsome young men, well, my tongue has been known to take on a mind of its own. When this happens, I put on the most contemptible of my many masks, that of the showman too full of himself and, more importantly, full of braggadocio. And the sight of the muscular arms of Michelangelo pushed me too far.

The young man sat listening patiently as I prattled on about my accomplishments since arriving at the Sforza court in Milan.

Like an idiot, I drank goblet after goblet as the dark-featured young artisan, handsome despite a broken nose, nursed a small cup of water. Finally, when I could take his stony silence no more, I asked him what *he* had accomplished in his young life. I swear on my mother's name, Cecho, I meant only to elicit conversation, but the young man, always quick to rise to a fight, took offense.

"Have you not heard of my *Pietà,* the one I carved out of a block of marble for the pope?" he asked, his dark eyes probing my golden ones.

"No, I haven't," I had to admit.

"Well, that's a pity," Michelangelo said. "Anyone who's a serious artist has. Or at least, those who can be silent long enough to hear about the work of others."

"*Ma, che cazzo,"* I spluttered, slamming my drink on the table. "How dare you say that? Don't you know who I am?"

To this, Michelangelo gave a wry smile, before saying, "I know enough about you to know that you rarely finish what you start. The colossal horse, the painting of Isabella d'Este, *The Last Supper,* even all those notebooks full of ideas and sketches…it seems to *me* that a serious artist should follow through with at least *some* of it!" he said, jerking out of his seat and moving to sit next to his friend Granacci.

"Well, at least I'm not just some stonecutter from a wretchedly poor family!" I yelled across the room.

LEONARDO'S LETTER

It was a terribly low blow. I should have guessed how sensitive the young man was about his family, who had come down in the world, and how he hated to be looked down upon by someone like me. It was common in those days for painters to disparage sculptors.

"I'm not some lowly artisan, *bastardo*," the young man spat. "I've read more than you." This was true, of course, as he had received a classical education, proud as his father was, despite how far the Buonarroti name had fallen.

"Well, here's a literary reference for you," I said. "May you burn in the seventh ring of Dante's *inferno*," I cried, evoking the insult used for men like us who sought the flesh of other men.

"You'll get there long before I do, *nonno*," Michelangelo said. "You're twice my age, yet only half as talented."

I slammed my goblet down and rose to my full height, but Salai and Boticelli suddenly appeared to place a hand on each of my shoulders and whisper calming words.

"Come now," Sandro said. "Everyone here knows you are the better artist. In fifty years, who will even have *heard* of Michelangelo Buonarroti? Meanwhile, *your* name will live throughout the ages."

"It's true, *maestro*," Salaì said.

I let their words soothe and calm me. "Perhaps I should just go home," I said, after a long moment. I suddenly felt quite tired and realized that it would be best to retire for the evening.

And so I did, hoping that the sting of the evening would quickly fade, and wishing to avoid the young stonecutter in the future. But, of course, Florence was not big enough for *that* to happen.

A few weeks later, when I was passing by the piazza in front of the Church of *Santa Trinità* by the Spini Bank, accompanied by Giovanni di Gavina, something happened that solidified our feud.

A group of notable Florentines who were discussing a passage by Dante asked me to stop and explain it to them. I was running late for an appointment with a friend who wished to discuss how flight could be achieved. This friend, like me, had been dissecting bats and studying how their wings could be copied for humans hoping to take to the skies. I had no desire to discuss literature that day, and, seeing Michelangelo passing by right then, I suggested that the men would do well to consult my young friend about the passage, as he seemed to know so much about the father of our language.

I swear that I did not intend sarcasm, nor did I mean for this to provoke anger; I was not even trying to be *cattivo,* but rather to send forth a small kind of peace offering, bowing to the young man's formal education, despite his rude appearance. I tried to appear jovial as I suggested that the gentlemen could learn something from the young sculptor, and honestly, I mostly just wanted to save time.

Also, truth be told, even though I have cultivated my mind through a great love of learning and perseverance, as I have already confessed, the study of letters has largely eluded me.

I was caught unprepared by the level of anger that my hot-headed rival was about to display, however.

"I'm not your friend. Explain it yourself, *stronso!*" he yelled across the street. "And while you're at it, explain to everyone why you were too lazy to finish your horse for the Duke of Milan!"

This was too much, because many of these men were part of the committee to decide what would be done with the so-called "Duccio Stone," a slab of white marble chosen by Donatello years before, and which I wanted for myself as a project to decorate our great Florentine Cathedral, *Il Duomo*. I had to stop and waste precious minutes explaining how Ludovico had used the bronze promised for my horse for cannonballs, afraid as he was of a French invasion. Little good it had done him, of course.

As everyone knows, my rival won this commission, and used that slab to create his masterpiece, the colossal *Davide*, that still graces a sacred place under the *Duomo*'s cupola.

At this late age, I am obliged to admit, grudgingly, that giving that chunk of marble to Michelangelo was the right decision, even if I cannot easily forgive him for sullying my good name in such a public way.

There are so many other examples of when I never finished a job. Why did he choose one where the fault was not mine?

I have lived for art, beauty, and creation. I have brought forth many things of which I am proud. I see it not as a fault, but rather a virtue, that some unworthy projects have, occasionally, failed to hold my full attention.

Oh, and the scorn of someone like Michelangelo? I wear it to this day like a badge of honor.

Arte Bellica

I guess now would be as good a time as any to return to an awkward subject… My dear Cecho, I assume you must have often wondered, but had too much tact to ask me why, as a good and decent man, did I lend my talents to developing the arts of war? Why work for the unscrupulous, or, to put it more frankly, at least in the case of Cesare Borgia, the despicable despot?

How did I go from designing ladders for the defense of Florence against her rival, Naples, during the Baroncelli conflict to designing huge crossbows and bombards? How did I go from painting angels for the *Baptism of Christ* with Verrocchio to imagining monstrous carriages edged with scythes capable of mowing down crowds of men? Even my meticulous and detailed maps were used for warfare by the Borgias.

The reason, of course, is simple, as I have stated before: beyond economic necessity, I wanted to explore where my mind could take me, whether in planning a splendid celebration, taking up the paintbrush to capture a pregnant mistress, or designing the most wondrous techniques or inventions that my engineer's mind could conceive of. Whether right or wrong, I chose to wash my hands of the consequences of my inventions and the products of my genius. I opted, when quite young, and when my life was threatened by the wagging tongues of jealous rivals, to follow my mind's fancies wherever they might lead, enjoying every step of the journey, ultimately taking no blame for what unscrupulous men did with what I created.

That is, until my time with Cesare Borgia. Even *I* have my limits with such things. Not that I did not take his money, though, and feel guilty about it later.

I like to think that the joy and wonder evoked by my paintings and other works of art could, in some small way, offset, in the great balance of things, the suffering I may have brought about.

It is true, I have come to believe; most of history, indeed, most of life, and that includes art, is composed of suffering. And I must not allow the anger caused by my suffering, for being disgraced and almost killed for that accusation of sodomy, to justify doing whatever I wanted, or some sad desire to prove people like Lorenzo di Medici wrong.

Although, I have often thought, what do I owe the world, one that would punish someone like me so, a man who wouldn't even kill a pigeon or a turtledove? As I have said before, it is hardly *my* fault that I am different.

Whenever I start down the path of justifying what I have contributed to, saying that I was only playing by the rules of a cruel world, I stop myself and consult my conscience, as well as my spirit. It is after doing this that I realize that such is not the essence of who I am. That is not who my uncle raised me to be.

I know, it is easy to judge one such as I, and you are probably right to point out my many hypocrisies. It is true, I chose not to sully my hands with the blood of any creature; I delighted in buying birds at the market and then setting them free, and then toiled away thinking nothing, at least at first, of designing machines of war for the evilest of men.

I call myself a humanist! I love and care for all men and women, you say, and you are right. How could my heart care more for the cooing creatures in a market square than for the thousands of men slaughtered by my trundling, armored cannons, and covered wagons ringed with guns?

Strangely enough, I have no good answer for this. To such criticisms, I can only shrug and say that you are probably right. However, in my defense, let me just say that I was simply applying the laws of motion and mathematics that I had mastered over many years of study, and for which I was paid handsomely. Not bad for an unlettered bastard from Vinci!

Would other men have designed machines of war like mine sooner or later? It may as well be I as another to receive the silver of an evil prince, such as the one Machiavelli was paid to write about. If what men like Cesare do with my inventions causes great suffering in this world, let those sins be placed at the feet of *his* soul, not mine. I am but a thinker, a simple man with a pencil, parchment, and a piece of chalk.

And, it must be said, most of what I designed has yet to be built, may *never* be made.

Besides, with a bit of luck, such inventions of warcraft might be used for keeping the peace. Some of my designs were purely for the defense of cities and fortresses, after all. Who is to say that, if war becomes too bloody in the future, inventions like mine may, in fact, *prevent* wars, once a period of intense bloodshed teaches men that armed conflict is something definitively to be avoided? Perhaps I will have done humanity a *service* by designing things that bring the evil of war to the fore.

Such musings and justifications help an old fool sleep at night.

In any case…mine has been a journey of discovery and of problem-solving, of following one passion to another until I ended my journey in this château, the guest of a French king and by the side of the dearest companion a man has ever known, my dear Cecho.

It has been a great life, and I have few regrets.

Men such as I, I have become convinced, were put on this earth as part of God's plan to fill the world with beauty and love, not for war and destruction. So let me spend my final days perfecting something of beauty, my masterpiece with the mysterious smile.

But on with the story. You were perhaps wondering about my time spent with and serving Cesare Borgia.

LEONARDO'S LETTER

I will not pretend that it was a good chapter in my otherwise storied career.

I first met the bastard son of Pope Alexander in 1499, as he was helping his friend Louis XII invade and take over Milan. I say the word "friend" generously, of course. A man like Cesare could never have anything like a true friend; for this type of man, who only thinks of himself in all things, uses his evil tongue to charm others and twist them to do his bidding. I suppose I must include myself in this list. I was bullied into serving the Borgia prince, it is true, but I would be lying if I claimed that I did not choose to serve him somewhat out of self-interest and thanks to his campaign of flattery.

If I am to speak honestly, I must say again that, like with Ludovico, who next to Cesare appears a choirboy, I was interested in exploring where my creativity could be taken under a wealthy and powerful patron. Of course, as with any Borgia, but with Cesare in particular, one should always sleep with one eye open, as today's favored servant is often tomorrow's inmate in a horrific prison, or worse, poisoned, burned, stabbed, or dangling from a hangman's noose.

Fortunately, Cesare was not the only one who knew how to play politics. Since time immemorial, men such as us have known how to stay alive through cunning, flattery, and, when necessary, deceit. Even as mad as Cesare was, he was, as they sometimes say among the English, "crazy like a fox." I was always more valuable to him alive than dead, so

I was able to keep my head on my shoulders while in his employ. In this way, I was not unlike my old acquaintance, Niccolo Machiavelli. He and I were nothing if not astute observers of human nature. I was better at imagining men in art, studying, painting, and dissecting their bodies, while Niccolo was better at observing how they get what it is that they want. I still hold that you can never know a man until you take a scalpel and cut into his flesh late at night in the basement of the castle of the dead. But that is for another entry.

I will never forget what it felt like when Cesare strode into *Santa Maria delle Grazie* that day in the fall of 1499. He had just helped King Louis take the city, and he wanted to tour the spoils of his conquest.

Despite Salaì's repeated and hysterical claims to the contrary, I felt it was still safe for me to stay in Milan, and trusted my instincts, which so far had rarely failed me. So it was that I stood touching up Judas's tunic and adding brown to Christ's sandals when I heard hoofs and footfalls on the cobbles outside of the church's rectory where I had spent so many years working.

I planned well for how I would look that day when Cesare would visit. I dressed in a sober, yet dignified, outfit befitting a man of my station; I wore red hose, leather shoes that were neither dirty nor too new, a clean blue tunic, and a rich gold-laced doublet that was expensive, yet not ostentatious. I wanted to give the impression of a successful gentleman artist and courtier, and the smile that spread across Cesare's face upon meeting me showed me that my carefully planned first impression had been a success. I looked the part!

Hoping to win a commission one day from his father, the pope, I made sure that *The Last Supper* stood before my guest in all its splendor, and that the thick curtains of the wide windows were parted just so in such a way as to cast heavenly sunlight on my creation.

Cesare was not a man of great faith — he had famously renounced his position as a cardinal and murdered his brother to lead the papal forces — but he knew a great work of art when he saw one.

"*Magnifico!*" he cried, praising my masterpiece, and pretending not to notice the bits of already-flaking paint. "But tell me, *maestro* Leonardo, you are a man who wields more than a paintbrush, are you not?" he said with a sly smile. "My agents tell me that you've done so much more than just *this* during your stay in Milan," he said, nodding at the painting of Christ and his disciples and dismissing it with a flick of his wrist. "I'm told that your magnificent clay horse, the one the French are taking pot shots at even as we speak, was meant to be a splendid bronze stallion. Pity that Ludovico used the bronze for cannons instead," he said with a rueful chuckle.

"As a matter of fact," I said, "I just so happen to have at your disposal today, a folio of designs and ideas for the arts of war," I said, feigning a casual air that belied my pounding heart and moist palms.

"My, my, you're a talented man," Cesare said, studying one of several pages on a clean table I had placed where I thought he might stand. "It's clear that you've put your study of mathematics and drawing to excellent use. Such a pity that Ludovico never knew how to use your genius to his advantage." He put the papers down, then studied me for a long moment.

"It seems that people have underestimated you," he said, coming to stand close to me.

"Thank you," I said, as Cesare drew even closer.

"You have a fine eye, Leonardo," he whispered, his breath almost on my neck.

"Indeed," I said, looking at the bag of silver that sat on the table before Judas in my painting on the wall.

"Your father…Lorenzo…Ludovico…certain *religious* authorities," he whispered menacingly. I shivered, thinking of The Prior. What had the man told this boy's father, the pope?

"None of them have ever truly valued you, or taken you seriously," Cesare said, his voice still barely a whisper. "Should you ever work for *me*, Leonardo of Vinci, I would never make such a foolish mistake."

I gulped, my throat dry, but nodded my agreement, my eyes again drifted upward to the bag of silver pieces before Judas.

LEONARDO'S LETTER

And so it was, although the deal would only be sealed years later, that I made a pact with the Devil that day in Milan. And the truth is, despite the fact that the earnings have allowed me to pursue great work since that time, including my beloved painting of the woman that I hope to get right before I expire…the truth, my dear Cecho, is that despite what I tell myself in order to sleep at night, I've regretted that decision every day since.

Bambini

Many have asked me if I ever regretted not having children, as most people like having their homes enlivened by the laughter of young people.

What can I say? I have never been a father, although I've had several young people in my life to whom I have been something of a paternal figure.

After Atalante left me, I was bereft for a time. My mother lived with me for a short time, but she was, of course, gone. Shortly before that, Salaì was entrusted to me as a child, and you know the rest, Cecho. That rascal was, of course, here with us in Amboise until a few months ago, but has since returned to the same vineyard his father worked when he was a boy. It is funny how some things, like my Vetruvian Man, can come full circle...

Although I never adopted Salaì formally, I did take him in and gave him a role to fill, namely that of my assistant. His parents hoped he would become a great artist, and it is true that I did what I could to teach him my trade. The truth is, however, that he was too much of a flighty little scamp, far too undisciplined (far worse than I, which is saying something) for me to be able to help him become anything but a spoiled and troublesome brat. However, if I am being honest, he did keep me company and help me often, especially at times when I found myself in need of a young person, and for that I am grateful, and plan to remember him in my will.

Some of the wagging tongues around Florence loved to speculate about what may or may not have gone on between me and Salaì. I can say, in all sincerity, that the boy was always simply my helper and my ward, and never anything more, although he had his share of fun on his own as a young man.

Of course, meeting *you*, my dear Cecho, has been the best thing ever to happen to me. Again, there were many who whispered ugly things about our connection, and about how much older I am than you, but who are *they* to judge if we have been happy? I wish everyone could find the love that we have had. You have been, Cecho, and continue to be, *l'amore della mia vita*, the love of my life.

One thing that I can assert with no reservations: I do not regret my lack of offspring. My work, my inventions, my paintings, my loves, and my friendships have all brought more meaning to my mad, wandering life than any children ever could have done, or at least that is how I feel now.

I have carried a bit of every place, every person, every lover, every bit of art, with me and hold all of these in my mind and heart. When I leave, I expect to bring all those things with me, and I will not be lonely. *Au contraire,* my dear Cecho, I will die a happy man, a fortunate soul.

STEVEN FARRINGTON

Volare

I have spent my entire life yearning for one thing, a single hope above all else; more than painting well, more than my dalliances with sculpture, anatomy, engineering, or my halting steps toward love…one dream, above all others, has dominated my febrile imagination.

The mad dream of flight.

Experience never errs; it is only your judgments that err by promising themselves effects such as are not caused by your experiments. Sadly, never was this truer than when it came to my dream of flight.

Many have asked me where this dream came from. I always respond that it came from my childhood. Wanting to know more, some have even asked me about my earliest memories.

My stepmother and mother both told me often that I gained the gift of speech early, at around the age of eight months, and that I was, in some ways, a kind of "talking baby," something that I myself find hard to believe, despite my precocious nature. However, they repeated this line so often that I find it nearly impossible to dismiss. Of course, if I truly had been an infant gifted with speech as they claimed, should I not then be capable of remembering vivid details of those tender months and years?

LEONARDO'S LETTER

In any case, I am wandering here, and I should, as the French are fond of saying, return to my sheep, and get on with my reflections.

My earliest memory is, perhaps unsurprisingly, that of a bird. A big, black bird, or so it seemed so at the time. Perhaps it was a crow, or a kind of vulture, or *nibbio* as we say around Vinci, which is a kind of kite or small, dark-colored hawk. I remember that I was in my bed, the window was open, the bird flapped its tail around my mouth, and then was gone as quickly as it had come, even though I cried out as if to die. The tail smelled like foul carrion, which follows, as these birds were, I learned later, occasional scavengers. I remember that I had to struggle for breath while it invaded my infant crib. This triggered my lifelong fascination for the winged creatures whose lives are full of such freedom that they come and go as they like, soaring high above the world.

A taste of death from a bird's tail made me want to defy the laws of nature.

Of course, the human mind is a complex thing, and who is to say whether this truly happened? Perhaps this was merely a story, a memory of a memory of a family story repeated so often that it became more lore than truth.

Of course, as we have been improving our French these many months, Cecho, I imagine you will laugh at how, even at a tender age, I had a tail in my mouth, knowing, as we do, the French slang of *"la queue,"* and what this word evokes here besides just the tail of a creature. Add to this the term for passionate release here is known as *"la petite mort,"* and this makes this childhood memory of a tail in my mouth evoking death and desire take on an even more interesting meaning.

It is true, I am a naughty old man. *Molto cattivo terribile.*

In any case, years later, as a child able to move around on my own, I remember perching on a hilltop not far from the cave that held the leviathan. I would spend hours on that outcropping of brown and black stone, watching eagles drift this way and that, fascinated by their ability to glide on the drafts of air, all the while alert and on the lookout for prey. Then, before my astonished eyes, they would spot something far below, some small creature perhaps, and flap and fold their wings to swoop, plummeting toward the ground at a great speed.

I resolved, as a boy, that I would someday discover the mysteries and laws of nature with the goal of mastering the art of flight for man and soar and dive like those birds.

Later, when I was a lad of nineteen and working for Verrocchio, I witnessed one of the most amazing spectacles of my young life. I was invited, shortly before his death, to a marvelous show of the greatest mind of Florence, Brunelleschi, as he reprised his marvelous theatrical presentation for members of the artistic guild of Florence, the *Annunciation*. I was invited to be one of the angels of this pageant, which was held at the Medici salon. The truth is that I was too afraid to try it, and besides, I weighed more than the other boys, most of whom were younger and smaller than I. These boys were dressed in golden robes and wings, and they brandished flaming swords as they swung from cables, thanks to an intricate system of pulleys and ropes, while the true star of the show, Gabriel, flapped gilded wings of his own and blew a brass horn as he hung aloft above a crowd of devils. I was not the only one left speechless that day at the sight of all these boys and men in flight.

Years later, in Milan, I was pushed to create a similarly extravagant series of spectacles, but I soon grew bored with putting all my creative energy into entertaining the Sforza court. I had begun dissecting dead birds and bats (I could not bear the thought of killing them myself, so I waited for ones that had already died), and soon I began to fill page after page with various observations about the wings, musculature, sinews, and everything I could learn about such creatures. I also recorded my mathematical observations and calculations about every aspect of flight. I spent long hours studying birds as they flew, and even noted how they took off and landed. More than anything, I wished to know how they stayed aloft. I wondered how the curves of their wings helped or hindered them, and how the speed at which they flapped their wings, coupled with their use of tails and heads, helped them maneuver through the air and navigate the wind.

Finally, in 1497, while still working on *The Last Supper*, I created the first of many inventions that I hoped would allow me to achieve my dream.

This first one was a re-creation of a large set of wings which I brought to Brianza, a small town nestled in the hills around Milan. I had been working for years on this system, a rudimentary flying machine, and I was so proud of it (although not as proud as I would be of various ones later in Tuscany). This one had bending, moveable wings like those of a bat, combined with the tail of a bird. Salaì was with me by then, and he accompanied me with some other young men to Brianza. We set Matteo, my volunteer, about a hundred *braccia* back from the edge of a crest overlooking a small pond. My thought was that, if the flight were to be unsuccessful, the fall would not be very far down, and Matteo would be able to land in the water, instead of on rock.

I wanted to be the one to test the machine myself, but my friends argued against it, and then Duke Ludovico himself forbade it, claiming that I was far too important, and my life and health could not be risked, unlike that of the young courtier from Genoa. Of course, I disliked the idea of *not* being the first in flight if my contraption worked, but I had to admit that I did not know how to swim and would be unable to save myself if I fell into the pond below, unlike Matteo.

The man was strapped to the middle of the machine, imitating the body of a small creature of flight, able to flap his wings thanks to leather straps placed under the appendages. With his feet, the pilot could manipulate stirrups attached in the rear, and he would move his legs as a runner does to generate additional flapping power for the large wings, in case his arms failed to generate enough of it.

I was convinced that the combination of light pine, cotton, and leather would allow man to fly for the first time ever, and that I would be able to offer up a real-life Ganymede to my friend Botticelli.

I spent the entire trip out to Brianza in a private coach with Matteo, even though my other assistants took my machine in another conveyance. I am lucky that Ludovico was willing to indulge me in such pursuits.

I meant to spend the entire time teaching Matteo how to move correctly so that he could imitate a bird, but the lad assured me that he understood right away, so I spent the rest of the trip trying to convince the young man to enjoy his time with me, as he might not survive the experiment. Sadly, he was not of a mind to try his hand at other adventures beyond the one of flight, so I had to resign myself to looking out the window at the beautiful Lombard countryside.

As can be expected, the experiment was a total failure. I cannot even claim that Matteo spent even one second in flight over the small body of water, although I maintain that I was able to fly for a few seconds years later off Monte Ceceri, near Florence. In any case, as Matteo was uninjured but cold and wet, he let himself be comforted and kept warm by me on my way back to Milan. In this way, my first experiment in flight was a failure, but at least I was glad to be able to hold and comfort a handsome fellow afterward.

Valentino

I would like to write a bit more on Cesare Borgia, but not much, as the less said about him, the better. He was a troubled soul, in a way that few men are.

Born in 1475, he was, of course, the bastard son of Rodrigo Borgia, who became, in 1493, Pope Alexander VI.

One way we know that things would be different during Alexander's pontificate was his willingness to recognize his illegitimate offspring, Cesare and Lucrecia.

From the start, we Italians were suspicious of the Borgias, Spaniards as they were. People dismissed them as Catalan parvenus — they were really from Aragon — but their foreign extraction should have been the *least* of our worries. Between the extravagant lifestyle at the Vatican, the blatant nepotism, the mistresses kept openly at court, the orgies, the murders, the naked desire for power, the gluttony, the conspicuous purchase of indulgences, and the total absence of religious underpinnings of that papacy have led to a great deal of well-deserved cynicism.

It is my understanding that a certain German monk has caused quite a stir recently in Wittenberg for his criticism of such papal excess.

LEONARDO'S LETTER

Dear Cecho, I know that you are a most fervent devotee of our Mother Church, and I would perhaps do well to allow her to clasp me to her bosom more tightly before I am called home to eternal rest; still, I admit that, even though I have yet to read Monsieur Luther's ninety-five complaints, I suspect that I would agree with many or most of them.

But, alas, back to that scion of the Borgia dynasty.

Cesare was, to my knowledge, the first man in history to renounce being a cardinal. Most men would be happy to be a member of that most powerful college, but not Cesare. After likely having his brother Giovanni murdered, he resigned to follow his quest for blood and power. His father decided to give him Romagna, putting the safety of Tuscany at risk. But first, he offered himself as *condottiero,* or mercenary, to the French King Louis XII, who named him Duke of Valentinois. As we Italians had a hard time pronouncing that, we just called him "Valentino."

It is strange, is it not, that such an innocent name, evoking love, should be given to such a devil?

As I mentioned before, Valentino had helped King Louis conquer Milan and the rest of Lombardy, and dislodged me from my idyllic life there, as the French would not have allowed a courtier such as I to remain there unmolested. My meeting him at Santa Maria Delle Grazie had sealed my fate, but I would only learn that much later.

STEVEN FARRINGTON

After my *parcours* through Mantua and Venice, I was happy in Florence, living among the Servite monks and working on paintings such as my *Salvator Mundi*, *Virgin and Child with Saint Anne*, and my *Virgin of the Rocks*, painted laboriously in oil on wooden panels. This was a happy time for me, as I obviously flaunted my nature in the face of the upright people of Florence, spurned my old friend Isabella in her quest for a personal painting, and spent my time exploring all sorts of hobbies and pleasures, such as chasing my old obsession of flight. And, of course, I tormented my ancient enemy, The Prior, every chance I got, knowing that my popularity with Soderini and aura of success protected me.

Of course, this joyous time could not last forever, and it was, ironically, my near success at mastering flight that led me, unwittingly, to the door, again, of that devil whom we called Valentino and his tempting offer that brought my soul to the gates of ruin.

Even though there are those who deny it, I maintain that I realized, at least for one glorious moment, my dream of flight, off the side of Mount Ceceri, in the summer of 1502. But no sooner had I done this, my wings were clipped for years to come. My fellow Florentines, perhaps out of jealousy, or expediency, pressed me into service for the Chancellery to keep Valentino at bay; of course, having some of Borgia's men there to witness the triumph of my flying "aerial screw" did not help, and soon Machiavelli and I were sent to Urbino, and then Imola. We were ostensibly called there to lead a diplomatic mission, and I was hired by

Valentino to be his military engineer, after he made me an offer I could hardly turn down, once his men had confiscated my flying machine.

I remember that autumn of 1502 quite well. Niccolò and I spent much of it holed up in the town of Cesena, where I designed a dam and a canal for my patron and maps of Imola and the Chiana Valley. However, along with the tools of war, and my fighting carriage ringed with guns, I ultimately regretted designing these for Cesare, as they helped him overrun the region of Romagna, and even hold my beloved Tuscany hostage. My guilt grew with each Borgia victory. While Niccolò observed and recorded every action and negotiation, ultimately using them for his now-famous treatise on how to acquire and hold onto power, I worked late every night, burning candle after candle, using up pages, chalk, pencils, and quills to design plans to help this evil man feed his lust for power. I cannot complain, of course, about my compensation; I earned thousands of florins for my efforts. But, as Our Lord said, what good is possessing heaven and earth, if one's eternal soul is in peril?

As a man of science, I cannot know where my soul will go after leaving this mortal coil, my dear Cecho. But one thing I *am* quite sure of, dear one, is that those months I spent working for Valentino were the worst days of my life, such was my spirit vexed and bereft of joy.

I have become convinced since then that people need a sense of connection to things of importance if they are to be happy and at peace. Being complicit with evil is *not* the way to feel closer to God, or to live a life of joy.

When I saw that my maps and designs were helping Cesare to conquer and kill, I began to realize that I could no longer, in good conscience, remain in his employ. When, on New Year's Eve 1502, he had a group of captains killed for no good reason, one of whom had become a good friend of mine, I knew that things had gone too far. Truth be told, I had been afraid to leave, but then I knew that staying would be far riskier, both for my spirit *and* for my health. I had to go. And I needed to convince Machiavelli to go with me.

And so that is what I did; in the middle of the night in early January 1503, Niccolò and I gathered up our things and hired a carriage, which took us back to the walls of our beloved Florence.

For a few months, the fear of retaliation at the hands of Valentino kept me awake at night. After all, I would not have put it past him to attack and capture our fair city out of a sense of revenge, despite Soderini's capable leadership.

However, luckily for us, Cesare had his hands full with occupying the tiny republic of San Marino. Then, in a stroke of luck for me and the whole world, Pope Alexander died suddenly in 1503. Despite Cesare's machinations, he was unable to regain control, and was soon forced to sail for Spain. He escaped from prison there, fled to Pamplona, and was involved in a siege of the town of Viana, where he was betrayed, stabbed, stripped, and left to die naked on the stones.

LEONARDO'S LETTER

I like to imagine him lying there as the blood and life force seeped from his destroyed body, looking up at the stars and wondering how it had all gone so wrong, how one so powerful could be alone and dying at the tender age of thirty-one. It was a fitting end for a murderer lacking in honor and compassion.

As for me, I gave away much of my ill-gotten gains from that time. I did not want to keep hardly any of it, preferring instead to donate and support the charitable aims of the friars among whom I lived. I considered it a kind of expiation of my sins.

I did, however, keep enough money so that I could dedicate my time and talents to finishing that altarpiece of the *Virgin and Child with Saint Anne*, as well as the painting of my lady, Lisa del Giocondo, the mysterious woman, the wife of a silk seller, whom I had spied at the market.

She was, and continues to be, my masterpiece, *il mio capolavoro;* she caps off a lifetime of effort on my part. She is the culmination of my skills and talents. Besides my love for you, Cecho, and the life we have built together, she is the thing I love most, my most precious creation, the one of which I am most proud.

I cannot be sure that my sins have, in fact, been expiated. Soon, my dearest boy, this silly old man will confess, take last rites, and close his eyes forever. However, I can take some small comfort in knowing that I have been the best artist, the best thinker, and the best friend that I could be, and hope that the balance of the good I shall leave outweighs the bad.

I hope not to spend much time in that seventh ring of *Inferno*; however, if I do so, I know that I will see most of my best friends there.

LEONARDO'S LETTER

Il Gatto Nero (The Black Cat)

I remember the day clearly, the day I saved Mirco, and gained a devoted friend.

It was none other than the Monday after I had returned to Florence, in January of 1503, after my disastrous time with *Il Valentino*. I had yet to fetch Salaì from the goldsmith with whom he had spent those months, living as a hopeless apprentice on the *Ponte Vecchio*. I had yet to don my silk tunics, fancy hose, and fabulously colored frocks from before; I was still wearing the humble attire I had used while in Cesare's employ — an amber-colored jacket, a black cap, and the simple brown breeches of a laborer.

I remember it as a warm and pleasant day, even though it was winter. A tepid sun shone through the clouds, and I had decided to go for a stroll through the narrow streets and piazzas near the Cathedral. Perhaps it was only my imagination, but I felt as if Florence did not welcome me back, and received me with suspicion; perhaps, I imagined, Machiavelli had whispered ugly lies about me, maybe even to the likes of The Prior, who could always be counted on to use information against me.

Of course, such thoughts were almost certainly just in my imagination; the more likely explanation is that

Florentines were going about their normal business, and I was just a sad and dejected old man.

I aged several years in the months I spent serving Cesare. My once beautiful face had finally begun to crinkle, and I had admitted defeat regarding the dying of my hair and beard, which were now almost completely white.

I walked past a wool market, where merchants were trading and hawking their wares. Florentines had become the most important importers of silks and dyes from the East, and the wool produced in our area was in high demand, with buyers as far away as England. This commerce, along with strong Florentine banking and the invention of that new style of accounting, had made our city only wealthier in recent years, and a strong merchant class had sprung up.

I walked past the shops of cobblers and decided that I was not in need of new shoes. I watched a blacksmith working at his forge for a while. Finally, I decided not to make the man feel self-conscious or belligerent when it became obvious how much I admired his muscular frame. He reminded me of the father of my onetime sweetheart, Lucia.

I kept walking, and before long, I found myself at the muddy banks of the Arno. Florence's river flowed lazily that day, and light danced and played off its surface. I studied, as so often I did, the little swirls and eddies of the water as I sat like a monk in quiet contemplation. Suddenly, a group of boys came running up with a small sack. They laughed and tossed the writhing burlap bag back and forth between them, and I could hear the cries of some scared creature coming from within.

"What do you boys have in that bag?" I demanded.

"Mind your own business, old man!" one of the lads snapped. He could not have been more than twelve.

"Che modi!" I cried, scolding him for his manners. In my day, children were always much more polite with their elders. "Who are your parents? Why are you tormenting some innocent creature?" I asked.

"Innocent?" the first boy scoffed. "Our *mamma* sent us here to *kill* this evil thing, a curse to our neighborhood!" one of the other boys called. "It's been lurking around all week, and it's sure to bring bad luck or witchcraft!"

"Don't be ridiculous!" I answered. "Now, which creature is it?" But I could easily guess. Florentines could be a superstitious lot.

"It's a dead one now!" called the third boy, as he tossed the sack into the river. With this, the boys turned and ran away, laughing.

I cursed, rolled up my breeches, and, without thinking, plunged into the icy waters of the river, my feet almost getting stuck in the mud. I suspected what I would find upon retrieving the bag.

Sure enough, a minute later, I found myself drying off a soaked black kitten. I tucked it into my cape, and soon its shaking subsided.

Not knowing what else to do, I brought the feline home and fetched some scraps and warm milk from the market. After eating, the tiny creature stretched out, yawned, and curled up in my lap as I sat by the fire. I confess that I spent the entire afternoon stroking and petting its fur, which finally grew warm and dry. I could not remember a time when I had felt more relaxed and at peace than I did when the fragile little beast first lay cuddled in my lap. When he opened his green eyes, the little cat studied me, and began licking my hand. I marveled at the tiny spikes and ridges on his little pink tongue. He purred loudly, and I wondered what made cats make this sound when they were happy. I studied his little legs and paws, all sinews, bones, and the tiny claws that nature had provided him. I wondered what made this little cat work. How did the blood flow in his veins? Did a pumping heart push blood all around his tiny body? How did his brain operate?

His tender body reminded me a bit of the bats I had dissected, but of course he was very much alive, and I intended to keep him that way.

It was so unfair, I thought, that such a lovable creature could be tortured and killed, just for being different.

What did it mean, I wondered, that even something like a cat seemed to display emotions such as joy and love? Because it was clear, at least to me, that this creature knew I had saved its life, and now had a bond with me, seeming to choose me, if not as its parent, at least as its caretaker.

Imagine Salaì's surprise when he returned to find a black kitten, with a small splotch of white on his nose, perched upon my shoulder. Salaì laughed at my foolishness, reminding me of what people would say, and questioning if I had enough time and patience to take care of a pet. I would not be swayed; this was *my* kitten now, and I would be damned if the wagging tongues of the friars or anyone else would make me give him up.

I named him Mirco, and he lived with me for the rest of the time I spent in Florence, before remaining with the monks when I moved to Rome, as they had finally grown fond of him too. He was a good mouser, and the brothers grew to see how useful he was for them, as their pantry was well protected. He was one of the best companions I have ever known, although he had a bad habit of curling up on top of my notebooks and cartoons and impeding my efforts when I tried to work in my studio. It was almost as if he were jealous of the time I spent on various projects, thinking that my time would be better spent feeding him leftover scraps from dinner or playing with him and some yarn. Perhaps he was right.

I must admit that I grew quite fond of Mirco. I still miss him. I grew to like him more than most people I have known. By now, fifteen years on, who knows if he is still alive? I like to think of him still catching mice, begging for treats, and then curling up on the laps of the brothers of the convent as they sit caressing his fur and relaxing by the fire.

Arte Sacra

Florence was not only a city of great painters and sculptors; she boasted an illustrious history of artists who created sacred art for many years, since at least the fourteenth century.

For a time, I had a kind of spiritual awakening myself during those years in Florence, and it is a feeling I have never completely lost, although my fervor has faded somewhat over the years.

I used to attend High Mass at our great cathedral, *Il Duomo*. I would pass admiringly through the brilliant doors, crafted by Ghiberti, and then I would look up at the amazing gold ball that Brunelleschi had placed on top of our great monument to God's glory. Never was I prouder to be a Florentine than when I found myself in that great place.

It is true; my spirit, in those days, dearly yearned for God, as well as it did for beauty. Just as one of my favorite psalms went, my soul thirsted for my God, as in a barren land without water. There was a song I heard at mass sometimes that went, *"sicut cervus desiderat ad fontes, sitivit anima mea,"* and the spirit of that chant resonated deep within me because, as the words went, my heart yearned for God, like a stag drawn to a fountain.

Sadly, I was a slave to two jealous masters: God and art. And while my confessor assured me that art was not a sin, and that I could love beauty as well as my creator, I never felt convinced. However, I did come to feel that art was a manifestation of something holy and good.

I sometimes thought of what Lorenzo *Il Magnifico* had told me all those years before, and now decided that he was right — a city filled with beauty most certainly *did* inspire a kind of public virtue. This was, I concluded, the case for Florence, even with the ugliness I often witnessed. Despite its problems, I still think that our Tuscan capital boasts the best character of people I have ever met.

On certain Sundays, I would wander down the Via del Sole to the parish of my favorite church, Santa Maria Novella. This I considered my home church, especially after my disastrous time serving *Il Valentino*. During mass there, when Father Giuseppe would say *"Pax Domini siit semper vobiscum,"* I really felt that he was speaking to *me,* calming *me*, and wishing that the peace of the Lord would stay with me always. When he sang his *Agnus Dei* in a deep baritone, I felt comforted, knowing that the Lamb of God had taken away my sins. When I told him my deepest secrets in the confessional, he always listened without judgment, gave me absolution, and told me that God loved me. It was the most soothing religious experience I had ever had.

It was then that I would repeat those words to myself again: "For the Lord will not cast off forever, but, though he causes grief, he will have compassion according to the abundance of his steadfast love…"

I always went to church alone, and my friends and other artists thought it strange that I did, as humanists often eschewed weekly mass. But I, on the other hand, felt the brush of God when I attended holy offices, and Father Giuseppe even encouraged my scientific explorations.

"When you understand the intricacies of God's creation, you know the beauty of His world, and appreciate Him even more, and such knowledge cannot be a sin, *carissimo*," he said.

Other times, I would simply enter the church at random, letting the silence of the place wash over me. Not only was this church a place of peace and tranquility, but it was also like a tour of Italian art from the thirteenth century onward. Its façade was by Alberti, and the treasures within had been made by Ruccellai, Messaccio, and many others. A crucifix by Brunelleschi graced an area up front, the side walls were covered with murals and paintings by Ghirlandaio, who had contributed a painting of the Birth of Saint John. The church, a minor Basilica, boasted of several small alcoves, such as the Strozzi chapel, a beautiful spot replete with various frescos and statues in gold and bronze.

The place was truly an island of beauty and calm. Sometimes, I would simply go in and sit, looking up at the high, ogive arches and the light shining in from the stained-glass windows on the nave.

I always knew I was safe from The Prior when I was in that church. He and Father Giuseppe were enemies, although I am sure that neither man would have admitted so openly. My enemy would never dare to darken the door of Santa Maria Novella, nor the convent attached to it.

After visiting this church, I always came away with a renewed sense of purpose, coupled with a greater desire to finish my altarpiece for the monks of the *Santissima Annunziata*.

Sharing the beauty of God's love for all through the gift of art was my purpose, my reason for being, the very thing that made me rise from bed alive and joyful every morning.

Other times, I would wander over to another nearby street, the *Via della Vigna Nuova,* where Alberti had designed various *palazzi* belonging to Florence's wealthiest and most prominent families. He was, indeed, the best architect our city had ever produced. I used to stop when no one was looking and peer through the laurel bushes and hedges, trying to catch a glimpse of the spacious gardens full of statues that had been excavated and brought to our city from ancient Greece, Southern Italy, and Rome.

How rich our history was, I mused, and how little I knew about it.

LEONARDO'S LETTER

Arte e Pintura

I spent a lifetime developing the art of painting, sometimes experimenting, innovating, or else following the steps and traditions laid out by those who came before me. I am deeply indebted to Verrocchio for everything I learned while in his workshop. Of course, I will never forget my favorite nugget of wisdom I learned from my late teacher:

"Leonardo, my boy," he said one day as we worked on the Adoration of the Magi, "learn the conventions and rules as well as you can, so that you understand the tradition fully, and know what you're doing. And then, once you have done so, you can *break* those rules as you make your way as an artist!"

This is what I have done, all throughout my life.

Some say that when my master saw me paint for the first time, he broke his paintbrush in two and swore never to paint again. This is simply not true. It is a fanciful anecdote that I never refuted, as it helped build my reputation and allowed me to find work. It never happened, Verrocchio continued to paint after he taught me, although less often. He *did*, however, often say that I had exceeded him as an artist, and I accepted the compliment, although perhaps I should not have.

Poor is the student who does not surpass the master.

STEVEN FARRINGTON

My father, my childhood tutor, and even my distant grandfather had always tried to break me of the sins of vanity and pride. They were unsuccessful.

There are some, mostly among the French, who think me the man who smashed all the rules of Italian painting. This, however, could not be further from the truth. Artists had been innovating and tinkering with techniques since Giotto, if not before, and there was at least a century of Tuscans pushing art past its traditional bounds before *I* was even born. However, I am delighted to be part of that pantheon of innovators, even though I am not the greatest by far.

This much, I *will* say: whereas before, painting was boring and flat, ruled by strictures of perspective and dull colors, we, in *our* century, brought about an artistic revolution. Simply put, we changed *everything*. Now, our palettes burst with colors, and our subjects shone forth from the shadows with a glowing force, imbued with divine light. We were nothing less than a priestly class, a breed apart that taught the world the beauty of God and brought His Word alive for a new age.

We artists of that time, instead of just painting how people had for centuries, innovated entirely. The figures we created were hard to tell from living, feeling men and women. We brought forth lifelike creatures whose inner worlds were real; we breathed authentic emotion into their every gesture. This allowed us to create dynamic, dramatic works whose characters compelled attention from those lucky enough to experience them. It went far beyond mere technique; we were in the business of reaching deep into our souls and pulling out what we found there to share with a world that needed to see it.

"If you bring forth that which you have inside you, it will save you," Verrocchio once told me. "However, if you refuse to bring forth that which you have inside you…it will destroy you."

Had I not followed the path I did, what would have become of me, Cecho? I do not know how I could have lived, had I never set out with my father to answer the call of destiny. Surely, had I wasted my talents in Vinci and never left that little corner of the earth, I would have become a wretched and frustrated man indeed.

But back to the painting, which is the real subject of this chapter, is it not?

We Tuscans shed the mantle of one-dimensional painting long ago. When I was young, it was still common to see painters following a Byzantine tradition, and then, of course, some, like my dear Isabella, who, it must be said, had more money than taste, insisted on those sideways portraits, as if my *contrapposto* were not good enough for her.

Many needed to be pushed to make their subjects occupy more than just one dimension. Some, like Ghirlandaio, wanted to paint saints in simplistic ways, while others, like me, knew that we needed to study the human body and nudes if we hoped to render bodies more lifelike and interesting. I always liked *chiaroscuro*, which had been developed by Florentines in previous decades, but not everyone cared to shade like that, preferring other ways to make bold contrasts between light and dark. I enjoyed bringing out the luminosity of my subjects.

Perhaps because of my being left-handed, I grew adept at making hatch marks that created tonal effects and shades of light in my sketches and paintings. I would spend hours making parallel lines and, sometimes, those at an angle to each other, to create the look I wanted.

I was always one to paint on a great variety of surfaces, of course. It could be a walnut panel, wet plaster, or even on a dry stone wall. I usually made my own oil pants by hand, using ground pigments, but sometimes I dabbled in other materials and techniques. Later in life, I made tempera from egg whites and worked on canvas, wood, or, if I was painting a mural, on stone, such as for my *Last Supper*, back in Milan.

Part of my process was to begin with an elaborate underpainting, a technique I learned while in Verrocchio's Verrocchio studio. This was usually in a neutral brown or gray. Once this was done, I would paint over it, and one could see through the other layers. At first, I didn't like the result, but then, Salaì came in one day and stood mesmerized by the effect.

''I can't stop staring at it, master," he said. "I can see the darker shades underneath, but the way you added the other colors and glazes over them, and it all kind of blends together…I just love it!"

I decided that, if a foolish boy like my assistant was fascinated by the effect of this technique, I must be doing something right. After all, almost nothing could hold his attention for more than a moment, or so it seemed.

It could be tedious and even mindless labor, but I always found it enjoyable and relaxing once I had begun. I admit that I was too often reluctant to start working, but once I did, my mind went to a place of such tranquility that I recalled my stepmother, Albiera, counting the beads of her rosary when I was small. Sometimes, I pushed late into the night because I enjoyed the art of mixing and painting. Once I got going, I could often barely tear myself away.

My life was such a crazy dash that painting was often a kind of escape. I could lose myself in my work for hours at a time.

I will say that, when I began my Lisa, everything changed. She is the culmination of my life's work. Every technique, every innovation of my art has gone into perfecting her. She is a real woman, living and breathing at my bedside just as sure as if Lisa del Giocondo were here at this very moment, in the flesh. I have spent so many hours staring at her, touching, retouching, and lovingly caressing her with my brush, as one would a lover. Sometimes, I even talk to her, and I would swear that she answers.

Although I have never asked you, Cecho, I am sure that you feel jealous of her, as I have, I am sad to admit, often neglected you for her on occasions too numerous to count.

I fear what will happen to her when I am gone.

It is true; I am never done with her, I am continuously revisiting her, my most beloved piece.

A painting is never finished, only abandoned.

I cannot abandon her. Not yet. This project of writing about my life, I could, and likely should, abandon soon, as it robs me of valuable time spent with Lisa and with you, Cecho.

Why can I not stop? What more can I say that anyone would possibly want to read?

In any case, I spent the years between 1503 and 1508 painting and enjoying my time once again in Florence, developing my skills as an artist. However, I knew that I could hardly stay there forever. Over half of my life was spent, after all, and I had never even been to Rome, except for one brief visit.

LEONARDO'S LETTER

Santa Anna, Maria, e il Bambino

Once I had escaped Cesare Borgia and returned to Florence, I threw myself into various projects. One of these was something I had begun before my mad adventure with the pope's son: I finally kept at, and then finished, my version of *Virgin and Child with Saint Anne.*

This painting is truly one of my favorites. It was for an altarpiece, but I always considered it something I did for *myself* and other devotees of true art, for it is a culmination of all my skills, a labor of love that was more than the sum of its parts.

This work became a kind of meditation, during which I retreated to my childhood for a time. After experiencing so much destructive masculine energy, I needed to commune with something of the *divina feminina* for a time, if only to heal my wounded spirit. It was like a salve for a heart broken by the cruelty I had seen at the hands of Cesare Borgia, who I still believe to have been an agent of the Devil.

It is true what you have heard, Cecho; I did indeed model my vision of Saint Anne after my long-departed stepmother, Albiera. I was horrified by the realization that I could no longer remember her face, but I did my best to evoke her patience and kindness in the countenance of that *madre divina,* as she accompanied Mary while the Blessed Virgin held, for her part, a writhing and squirming baby Jesus. Of course, I used the memory of my dear mother, whose beauty was unmatched in women, for this figure. She had joked that the greatest aspect of having an artist for a son meant that she could be immortalized in art, and so I am glad to have granted her this wish, albeit posthumously.

Of course, I know what you must be thinking, dear Cecho: how dare I compare *myself,* a great and flawed sinner, to Our Lord, if, necessarily, my mother being Mary, then *I* must perforce be like the figure of the blessed babe. Well, rest assured, *amore mio;* far be it for me to stoop to something like that (and how could I know what I looked like as a baby, in any case?). No, the cartoon and subsequent image of the infant in the painting was drawn from many composite sketches of various newborns I observed in the markets of Florence, whom I sketched surreptitiously as their mothers shopped.

Every time a child is born, my dear one, is it not a kind of miracle? Jesus was, of course, human, the Word of God made flesh of man, *Lumen de Lumine, Deum verum de Deo vero, genitum non factum,* etcetera. But I believe that every child is a kind of miracle given to us by God. And my many years of study of the human machine have not diminished this belief one iota; if anything, the exploration of science has only *strengthened* my mystic belief in the divine.

LEONARDO'S LETTER

In one of my original cartoons, I designed Our Lord as reaching out to hold onto John the Baptist. However, upon further reflection, I thought about what The Prior would whisper about such a depiction — a boy with two mothers reaching for another boy! It was enough for the wretched Prior to have me jailed yet again, if not sent to the burning stake. (I realize that this is perhaps unlikely, but why take the chance if a lamb would do just as well?)

I worked on this painting, off and on, for years. When the work came to an end in 1507, I sat for a long time, contemplating my creation.

I know that pride is one of the seven deadly sins, Cecho, but I will freely admit that a wave of that unsavory emotion washed over your dear Leonardo upon viewing the work that I finally had to deem finished. I scarcely knew how such a piece of priceless beauty had swept from my humble brushes.

I had created a spiraling pyramid of divine, mostly feminine, motion. The bodies were entwined with each other, full of dynamic, loving energy; the gazes and forms communicating love, and even something like fear, as Mary must have known that her son would eventually sacrifice himself for all humanity, as the lamb he reached for symbolized.

The figures were of an exquisite, glowing beauty, a divine spirit that gleamed forth from the shadows. They were both human and beyond humanity, flesh and divine energy brought together in one swirling, spiraling, ever-moving dance.

The background showed itself as a muted bluish gray, somewhat hazy atmosphere, evoking a time of innocence and tranquility, much like my beloved childhood in the Vinci countryside, a place that had faded into a gentle and soft dimness in the foggy, misty corners of my mind.

It was then that a realization came to me.

Now that I had drunk deeply the elixir of life, I knew that it was time to go back home for a visit.

LEONARDO'S LETTER

Volta a Vinci (Return to Vinci)

I cut quite the surprising figure as I returned to Vinci in the year 1507.

I had become a famous and successful artist. I had wealth, power, and prestige. I could dress as the successful gentleman I had become, sporting expensive hose, silk tunics, gold-embroidered doublets, and even a jaunty felt cap with plumes that I used to cover my graying (or white), yet full, head of hair and beard.

It was a double surprise that I came back with a young man whom I had adopted, even if informally, who was such a rascal and a nuisance as Salaì, and that a black cat followed me everywhere I went. However, when you are a successful and famous painter, engineer, and courtier, I have learned that people overlook such eccentricities, and my visit to my home village was no exception.

My uncle Francesco was an old man by then. He was no longer able to work the farm as he had when he was young, but he had a few servants and laborers who did the chores for him, as well as some money my father and grandfather had left that allowed him to live comfortably.

I had been out to see him once or twice before leaving for Milan, but I think the last time would have been in 1480 or so. We had exchanged letters over the years, especially since my father's death in 1504, when my uncle and several other relatives came to his funeral in Florence.

"It's so good to see you, nephew!" Uncle Francesco said, embracing me. His cheerful green eyes were the same, crinkling with joy and kindness around a sea of lines caused by a lifetime of laughter.

After lunch, I asked him to read me something from his library, as he used to do when I was a child. He always found the most beautiful poems and words of inspiration for me. To my surprise, he opened a new Bible that he certainly did not have when I was a boy, a beautifully printed version of the sacred text from Venice with colorful illustrations and glorious woodcuts. He looked up at me, smiled, and told me that he thought I would like this passage from Isaiah. He read aloud:

"As the rain and the snow come down from heaven, and do not return there until they have watered the earth, making it bring forth and sprout, giving seed to the sower and bread to the eater, so shall my word be that goes out from my mouth; it shall not return to me empty, but it shall accomplish that which I purpose, and succeed in the thing for which I sent it. For you shall go out in joy and be led back in peace; the mountains and the hills before you shall burst into song, and all the trees of the field shall clap their hands. Instead of the thorn shall come up the cypress; instead of the brier shall come up the myrtle; and it shall be to the Lord for a memorial, for an everlasting sign that shall not be cut off."

LEONARDO'S LETTER

I sat for a long moment with my eyes closed, savoring the beauty and the poetry of the passage. Finally, I opened my eyes, and my uncle looked at me knowingly.

Like the words in the passage, I had gone out in joy as well as in trepidation, but had been led back in peace to this lovely place where I had spent my childhood. And in my joy of returning home, I felt as if the trees and hills greeted me as a beloved son.

"Let's go for a walk around the farm and the village while we catch up," my uncle said, and so we did.

After having visited and lived in so many cities, I was struck by how small and provincial Vinci seemed, how quiet and peaceful it felt. I had become used to the hustle and bustle of an urban setting, the constant sound of carts, cries of vendors in the market, and neighbors calling back and forth to each other across chaotic alleyways. The lack of such things was truly a shock.

"You've become a real success, *nipote*," he said with a slap on my back, and I felt sad for not visiting him sooner. "You've been painting and inventing such marvelous things, even *we* have heard of your triumphs all the way out here," he said with a grin that showed how proud he felt.

"A lot of it is thanks to you," I said, turning to smile at him. "I never really *did* thank you properly. You were more of a parent to me than my own father."

"Seeing what you've become is payment enough for me, Leonardo," he said. "And it was with great pleasure that I helped raise you."

"Did you ever regret not having children yourself?" I asked. "You never married…"

"Well, *nipote,* let's just say that you and I have more in common than you may have realized," he said with a wink. "I knew love when I was young once. And then, when I was able to, I was overjoyed at the chance of taking care of you as a boy."

"Grazie, zio," I said, giving him a hug. It felt good finally to embrace him.

Then, recognition finally dawned on me; my father had taken me away from this kind uncle who had never married because he feared I would end up like him. How funny it was, however, that he had sent me to live with artists and humanists instead, who were the most likely men ever to engage in what my father feared.

The next day, I walked over to the hamlet of Anchiano, where I had spent those first few years with my mother. She was gone, as you know, and the humble house lay empty. I inquired about a distant uncle and older cousins, but it turns out that they had passed on a few years before. I was able, however, to visit with some of my step-siblings. They were, without exception, humble country folk who had barely heard of me, which was fine.

LEONARDO'S LETTER

I decided not to go exploring deep into the hills around my home village. Part of me even feared that the "monster cave" had never existed at all, and that I had imagined the whole thing.

I wanted to preserve those memories of my happy childhood. I did not want those places to seem disappointing or small. I hated the idea of those craggy hilltops, from which I had watched the diving eagles, seeming less than the majestic places that still lived on in my mind.

What if all of it had been merely dreams, figments of an overactive imagination, or, worse yet, false memories?

I spent several days back in Vinci with my uncle, and he and I had several conversations that went deep into the night in his library. I enjoyed that visit very much, and during it, I realized how much of the person I had become was thanks to this kind and inquisitive man.

I will speak of one final conversation I had with him, which was about a homily I had heard as a child with him in our little country church from the priest who had, for a time, been my tutor.

"Do you remember, Leonardo?" my uncle asked. "That parable about the fig tree?"

I nodded, recalling how my uncle had often returned to this when I was a child.

"The owner of the fig tree wanted to cut it down, as it wasn't producing any fruit," he said. "But the gardener asked for more time before it would be felled..." He paused. "He believed in the little tree, knowing that it just needed a bit more time, a bit more care, before it would produce the desired results. He advocated for the fig tree, seeing its potential, hoping that the owner would spare it until it could do what it was meant to do."

I nodded once again, fighting back tears.

My uncle had been my gardener, my advocate, my greatest nurturer.

That would be the last time I would see him. I have been grateful, and I have never forgotten him.

LEONARDO'S LETTER

The Spiral Dance

One place I visited before returning to Florence was the little stream at the bottom of the hill by my uncle's home. I was delighted to see a little bridge that someone had built in the years since my departure.

Mirco followed me down to that bridge, but when I stepped onto it, he meowed plaintively, possibly due to the fear of water he had ever since his rescue as a kitten. I scooped him up, and he nuzzled my face before hopping onto my shoulder.

I stood for a long time peering into the water below. I saw the image of an old, gray-haired man in a stylish doublet and a well-groomed beard staring back at me. I realized that the last time I had peered into this stream, I had been a boy of twelve, a lad of golden eyes and curls. I had had my whole life in front of me then. And that memory seemed so close, I could almost reach out and touch it.

I studied the curls in my gray hair and beard, and then watched the spirals in the water as the eddies swirled all around. The water seemed to bounce happily off the rocks and pebbles in that stream as it made its way to the Arno hours away, and then, eventually out to the sea. I looked at the big rock in the middle of the stream, then thought of how many problems I had had to go around, like the flowing, eddying water.

My lifelong fascination with spirals, ranging from the curls in people's hair, to the shapes found in water, paint, and even my flying screw — this fascination had been born *here*, and here I was once again, studying the eternal dance of shapes and forms the way I had as a boy.

Far from fearing a flood, I enjoyed the peaceful feel of the place. I breathed in the cool fresh air and studied the water again.

I wondered if some of the water I had spied as a child had made it to the sea and then kept going, perhaps even as far as the New World discovered by the Spanish and Portuguese a few years before.

How vast and interconnected our mysterious world is.

The Prior, Again

Of course, I returned to Florence, and spent several more years painting before heading to Rome. Those were good years. My reputation as an artist grew ever more, and soon, powerful people all over the peninsula had heard of me.

However, you can by now imagine who came to interrupt my felicity.

It was shortly before I was to head to Rome. My fame was at its height in Florence, and I had never felt better. My spirit felt like it could soar, even if the dream of sustained flight still eluded me.

So, naturally, that is when The Prior arrived, yet again, to torment me and bring me down to earth. Only this time, it was not at the market, and it was not only me. This time, I was sitting with some friends in a tavern, enjoying some wine, when the man showed up and decided to bother me yet again.

He must have been walking past the tavern door and looked in, because, before I knew it, he stood next to me, looking quite out of place in a locale where one would never expect to see a man of the cloth, much less one such as he.

"*Master* Leonardo," he said, a sneer in his voice. "I see you are enjoying yourself in a place of excess. This should surprise no one."

I sighed. "What do you want?" I asked, showing absolutely no deference to the man who had tormented me for my entire adult life.

"Nothing. I'm just here to remind you that Florence is still a *Christian* city, and that I have my eye on you and your sinful ways."

I slammed my fist on the wooden table, making my tankard jump. "Are you accusing me of something specific?" I demanded, glaring up at the old devil.

"Nothing...*specific,*" the old man said, his lips sliding over his teeth as he said the word. "But...you are a strange bastard, an unmarried artist with a fine eye who lives with a boy, a black cat, and writes with his left hand, are you not?" he asked. "All odd things for a man. Signs that point to...other things. It would be a shame if the Inquisition were to look closely into your affairs..."

"Leave him alone," came a voice from behind me, and I was shocked to see someone unexpected rise to my defense from the table behind us. I had not noticed him, as he had been sitting with his back to me. He stood now in a simple artist's smock, his cheeks marked by dark stubble, his bare arms rippling with a working man's muscles.

"Michelangelo Buonarroti," The Prior said, stepping back and taking the young sculptor in with hungry eyes.

"It's been quite some time since I've seen *you*. You've grown into quite the man." He paused before adding, "It's been *quite* some time. Perhaps you should come see me again, for confession. Otherwise, I could pay your father a visit. And we wouldn't want *that,* now, would we?"

Michelangelo's eyes burned with a quiet rage while he stared the old man down, so much so that I imagined that everyone present wondered why, what possible history the two could have between them.

"Leave this place. Leave it at once, or I will tell," he growled, his voice barely above a whisper.

The Prior just laughed before turning to leave the tavern. At its door, he turned, looking at a room full of artists, taking us all in and attempting to smile, but treating us to a disturbing grimace instead.

"Just who, exactly, do you think they would believe?" he asked, before leaving.

STEVEN FARRINGTON

Mona Lisa

Just as I had met my worst enemy at the market, so did I meet my greatest muse there as well.

It was late spring. I had been back in Florence for several months, working on my *Virgin and Child with Saint Anne* for the Servite monks, and I decided to do some shopping. I wanted to experiment with some new dyes and oils, as well as tempera, for which I needed egg whites, among other things.

I was meandering through the market stalls, and my eyes fell, as so many times before, on a group of doves who looked unhappy in their captive state. As I have done a few times in my life, I plunked down several *soldi,* and the vendor looked at me as if I were mad as he scooped up the coins and nodded toward the three white birds cooing in their wicker cage.

I opened the door of the small, wooden prison and watched with delight as the birds flew away. As usual, I studied their beating wings, and I wondered, for perhaps the thousandth time, how they were able to master flight. If these tiny creatures could do so with their simple, tiny brains, then why couldn't I?

"I should like to fly away like that," said a voice behind me as I stood with my face upturned and graced, sadly, with what I imagine was a foolish grin. I turned around, and that was when I first laid eyes on her. She was not the most beautiful woman I had ever seen, but certainly one of the most intriguing. What I noticed, after her face, were her gentle hands that rested on an ample, and obviously pregnant, belly. Her hair was held in place tightly by pins and combs encrusted with numerous pearls and jewels. Her skin was of an almost luminescent olive complexion. Her eyes were full of wisdom and curiosity. Her lashes and eyebrows had been almost completely plucked, as was the fashion for upper-class women of Florence of that time.

There was something about this woman that I could not quite put my finger on, a unique element so captivating and compelling. Had I dreamt of her? I felt that I knew her already, even though I could not recall ever meeting her before, at least not during my waking moments.

But the most memorable aspect about this incredible woman was her smile. It tugged mysteriously at the edges of her lips. I wondered what lay behind it. It hinted at a spirit touched with joy, yet also tinged with sadness, as if she had been disappointed by life, though she still held out hope for things, perhaps, to get better.

"I believe you will achieve your dream of flight like those birds one day, Signor Leonardo," she said, a slight smile creeping again onto those lips, her dark eyes twinkling before she turned away.

"Signora...aspetti, per favore, aspetti un attimo," I called after her, hoping that she would wait and let me talk to her, but she disappeared into the crowd.

Who was that woman with the enigmatic smile? And how had she known about my dream of flight?

A few months later, I found myself once again at the market, on the hunt for new materials and dyes for my paints, which I was always tinkering with. I was exploring the aisle of silk merchants when I spied her; she had given birth, and now held a baby to her breast as she sat placidly in a booth next to a man who was, presumably, her husband.

The man looked much older than she, perhaps twenty years her senior. It was not uncommon to see widowers remarrying after their wives passed away, especially in childbirth; after all, my father had made it to a fourth wife, and this man, Francesco Giocondo, was on his second, as I was to learn later.

I tried not to look at his lovely young bride and mother of his *bambino* as I introduced myself. As luck would have it, the gentleman, a successful silk and cloth merchant, knew who I was, and seemed impressed. The two of us engaged in a lengthy discussion about colors and dyes, and I made it known how keen I was to get my hands on some of his best materials, so I could do a better job on the altarpiece for the friars (as it turned out, he had seen my popular cartoon for it the year before).

"There is, however, the awkward question of the price of these materials," I began. "The Servite brothers have been unable to pay me just lately," I lied.

"That is difficult indeed," Giocondo replied, stroking his graying beard, the feather quivering jauntily atop his velvet cap.

"Perhaps we could come to some kind of arrangement," I said. "You may know that I've painted many portraits, especially of several distinguished ladies," I said obliquely, taking the chance of looking past him at his lovely wife.

The man studied me for a long moment. I held my breath, hoping that his natural Italian jealousy could be overcome by a desire to have a portrait done by a famous artist, and that he would be placated by what I assumed was the common knowledge of my preference for the company of men.

"Well," Giocondo said after a long moment, "I shall have to discuss the matter with Lisa first. But we *are* moving into a larger home soon, and I would *so* enjoy having a painting of her, especially since our son Andrea was recently born."

"*Congratulazioni,*" I said, tipping my cap to the man and to Lisa. "In that case, I will return here next week to see how the matter stands."

"*Bene,*" Giocondo said with a slight bow, and I caught a glimpse of his wife before I turned away. There was that smile again, which had crept back onto her voluptuous lips.

*

Not long after this, I was invited to the family's new home on the Via della Vigna Nuova, and Lisa and I sat on the large balcony overlooking a spacious yard. Her husband had left us alone, but a servant came to check on us every few minutes.

Lisa occupied a *pozzetto*-style armchair. She sat between two columns that were one of the hallmarks of the Alberti style of design, as the new merchant classes tried to make their homes look like the villas of Ancient Rome.

Salaì sat nearby on the edge of the balcony, and I begged him to be on his best behavior. I threatened to send him away for good if he pilfered so much as one of Lisa's pins or pearl-covered combs.

Despite the pleasant weather, and the fact that she was about to have a portrait made of her by one of Florence's most renowned artists, the lady, whom I addressed formally as Madonna Lisa, looked melancholy. She had dressed in her best crème-colored gown, and her hair was pinned perfectly into position.

"Are you going to begin the portrait today?" she asked. "I don't see any of your paints."

"No, Madonna," I said, setting a large sheet of beige paper on an easel and fixing it in place. I took out my charcoal pencils. "Today, I will simply make a cartoon of you," I said. "A *sketch*," I corrected myself, knowing that I should avoid specialized terms.

"I know what a cartoon is," she answered, a gentle reprimand in her voice.

"Of course," I said, wondering a bit about her reply. This young woman had had a life before marriage, albeit a short one. What could it have entailed?

"You are not the first artist I have known, Leonardo," she said reproachfully, her eyes twinkling with mischief. "Nor are you the first to want to capture my likeness."

I was unsure of how to respond to this, and I did not wish to be indiscreet. Nevertheless, I found myself drawn even more to this woman upon hearing this. She reminded me in some ways of my old friend Cecilia, of whom I'd painted *Lady with an Ermine* back in Milan, and her confident spirit made my mind harken back to Isabella d'Este. Of course, I had always resisted painting Isabella; perhaps I now found myself painting this portrait of Madonna Lisa that I always should have wanted to do of the Marquise of Mantua. I would show her as a vivacious, intelligent, confident young woman, painting her facing the viewer, at three-quarters view, so that anyone seeing her would be struck by her vivid and undeniable humanity.

Once I had my cartoon of her, I began work, during my free time, on the first painting of the lady. However, I mostly kept this, done on a poplar panel, in my rooms at Santissima Annunziata. Of course, I would revisit the lady at her home periodically over the next three years as the painting progressed, especially the first one.

On my second visit, Lisa wore a more comfortable dress that hung off her shoulders. While I was finishing her cartoon, Salaì played with her son in his crib, dangling a piece of yarn over the baby like he used to do with Mirco when he was a kitten. I saw it for a fleeting moment: the vision of those wistful, mysterious upturned lips I had witnessed the first time Lisa and I had met, the day I had freed those birds at the market.

Suddenly, I was seized by a burst of artistic inspiration.

"Madonna," I began, "would you humor me for a moment?"

"Certainly," she replied.

"Would you please remove your hairpins and your combs?"

Lisa looked a bit dubious, but she did as I asked. Soon, a dark mane of hair cascaded around her beautiful, bare shoulders and down along her back. The hair framed her lovely round face and her enigmatic smile.

"*Brava*," I said, picking up my chalk and charcoal pencil, taking up a new piece of paper and beginning a new sketch.

I worked on this second sketch for some time. Soon, I discovered that I liked her more this way, without her adornments, her hair falling naturally in a comfortable, simple dress. She seemed happier too, freer, more herself.

After a while, her smile grew into a gentle laugh. "Do you intend to paint me this way instead?" she asked. "My husband would hardly like *that*."

"And why is that, my lady?" I wanted to know.

"Well, it's just that…these combs were a gift of his, and he finds me especially beautiful when I wear them and with my hair up. He says that it displays my features better, my…bearing."

"Hmmmm," I said, not knowing how to respond. Her husband was certainly correct in that which he described as the fashion of the day.

Lisa's lips lifted slightly upward again. "Just what are you thinking, Leonardo?" she asked.

"I am thinking, my lady," I began, "that, with your permission, of course, I would very much like to paint *two* portraits of you," I said.

"Oh?" she replied, a look of surprise crossing her face.

"Yes," I replied. "One would be, naturally, the version your husband desires," I said. "That one would show you as *he* likes to see you and think of you. It would be in formal dress, wearing your pins and combs, framed and contained in those Romanesque columns, almost as if you were a bird in a cage. The background would show a perfectly harmonious Roman garden full of cypress trees or myrtle, perhaps even some statues. Maybe one of Venus. A proper, beautiful merchant's wife with barely a trace of a smile."

She looked at me as if she were complicit with my plan already. "And the second one?" she asked, her eyes showing a hint of excitement, but also nervousness.

"The second portrait would be of how *I* see you. Especially how I see you *now.*"

She held her breath for a long moment.

"And how is *that*, Master Leonardo?"

I looked up from my sketch, smiled, then reached out to the cartoon. I wetted my finger and began to blend and shade the shadows around her eyes with the charcoal, giving the illusion of smoky shade and a sense of mystery that we Florentines have lately taken to calling *sfumato*.

"The second painting will be just for us. Just for *you,*" I said. "It will depict you as you sit now, with your hair down, wearing a dark Florentine dress, the kind you might wear here at home. You will be shown as comfortable, confident, and intelligent, a person full of mystery and depth."

She said nothing for a while, and seemed to contemplate what I had just offered her. I imagine that she wondered if her husband would be upset to find out that there had been a second painting done of his wife without his consent. What if it were displayed publicly without his knowing? There could be a scandal.

"And the background of that second painting?" she finally asked.

I smiled, suspecting that she would agree, or at least consider what I had proposed.

"Gone would be the Roman columns or a decorated background," I said. "Instead, it would be of the wild Tuscan countryside, like the one where I used to play as a boy. I grew up near Vinci. Do you know that place, or one like it?"

She nodded, as I knew she would. I decided not to probe further. I enjoyed the fact that Lisa kept her mysteries to herself.

She seemed like one who had had an untamed childhood, much like mine, before having to suppress that playful side to please a husband who wanted his wife and the mother of his sons to behave as a proper lady should.

"We shall call the second one *La Giaconda*," I said, with a laugh, delighting in the pun hidden in plain sight. Not only would it be the feminine form of her husband's name, but it would reflect her discreetly hidden — unless one sought it out — jocund and playful side that most would not be able to see unless they chose to study her from a different angle, as I was doing now.

In fact, in this second portrait, I would use all my knowledge and gifts as an artist and as a student of nature. I would use mathematics, anatomy, light, shadow, and perspective, to show what only some viewers would be able to see, should they make the effort. Unlike my work in Milan, this work would just be for Lisa and for me, at least for now.

Looking straight at her, as I imagined her husband did, most viewers would only see a conventional woman.

Her smile, and the magic in her eyes, would only be revealed to those willing to look at her another way. They would have to use their heart, their imagination, to see what I saw.

And for those able to do so, her smile, and her eyes, would follow them, haunting them, as they still do to me to this very day, even when I am not studying her second painting here in the room with me at the Chateau at Amboise.

Years after her untimely death, Lisa's smile, her eyes, and her very spirit, follow me still.

Diverting the Arno

Another project that I should mention from around this time is my attempt to change the course of the Arno River.

Macchiavelli approached me soon after we both got back from our disastrous time working for Cesare Borgia. Niccolò had been impressed with my many ideas for war, such as the one about horse-drawn chariots that could attack the enemy with whirling scythes, something that Cesare only tried once, thanks be to God, and the one time I witnessed the destruction caused by this idea, it gave me nightmares for years afterward. Therefore, you can understand my hesitation when Niccolò approached me in a tavern one day and asked me to attend a meeting with him and the council of men, known as the *Gonfaloniere Signoria,* who had succeeded Soderini in the Palazzo Vecchio.

By that time, I had finished the *Saint Anne* project and was working on a mural for the city hall depicting the Battle of Anghiari, so it was not much effort for me to come to a meeting held in that same building where, as it happens, we both worked anyway.

"I'll get right to the point," the head of the council said once pleasantries were dispensed with at the meeting. "We're at war with Pisa," he said. "Or we might as well be."

I groaned upon hearing this. Did they want me to design more contraptions to kill soldiers in battle? I had had quite enough of *that*, no matter how interesting such problems might be to figure out.

"Thank you, *signori*, but I fear I will have to decline your kind offer," I began. "My days of designing the implements of war are over. I plan to dedicate my final years to painting," I said, turning to leave. I decided against mentioning my long-held dream of flight.

"Leonardo!" Macchiavelli called as I had nearly reached the exit. I turned around to listen, against my better judgment.

"We don't mean to waste your many great talents on something so *trivial*, so beneath you, as *warfare*," Macchiavelli said, the feather in his cap quavering slightly as he spoke. "No, we have a special project that we hope you might be keen on helping us with. In fact," he said, knowing me well enough not to push too hard, "in fact, this project, which only *you*, Leonardo, are clever enough to make work, would be completely peaceful and would likely *forestall* direct warfare were it to work, as it is a manner with which we could strike against our downriver enemy without resorting to bloodshed. In fact, by helping us, you would likely be *saving* lives."

LEONARDO'S LETTER

Damn him, that Niccolò. He knew exactly how to get me to do what he wanted, sensing, as he did, my remorse for the deaths I had helped bring about at the hands of Cesare Borgia. That, I thought ruefully, and an appeal to my vanity.

I sighed, came away from the door, and sat down at the table where the men laid out their plan, which sounds mad even as I write it here. They hoped to divert the river Arno, send its waters into another basin, and thus deprive Pisa of their water supply.

It would never work, I told them. It was sheer madness even to consider, much less attempt, such a project, I said.

However, they appealed again to my pride as an engineer, and I must admit that I was seduced by the idea of trying such a project, the likes of which had never been done before.

Before long, and despite my numerous misgivings, I had devised a plan to, in fact, divert the great Tuscan River.

Soon, we had thousands of Florentine workers, some of whom were from Michelangelo's family, constructing a dam and digging a new course for the river. However, through no fault of *my* plan, and against my advice, a new channel was tested before it was ready, and this test coincided with a great rainfall, the worst in decades to hit Florence.

I am sad to report that the dikes and dam burst, the water went every which way, and there was great flooding everywhere in Florence.

Since the time of my childhood, I have been obsessed with the idea of a great and destructive deluge. This disaster was, of course, the worst flooding disaster I have ever witnessed firsthand, and it gives me nightmares to this very day.

No one blamed me. Well, no one besides Michelangelo, whose brother was just barely rescued from drowning the day the dam broke.

Oh, and of course, The Prior yelled from his pulpit and to anyone who would listen that God had, once again, as with Noah, sent a horrible flood to punish the sinful and prideful ways of the men of our city who had turned their backs on him. He had special condemnation for me, as you can imagine, although stopped just short of accusing me personally, by name, of sins against God and nature.

The city council canceled the project, and tensions with Pisa subsided on their own.

LEONARDO'S LETTER

Other Beloved Projects and Paintings

During those years following 1503, and especially following the failure with the river diversion, I decided to focus again on painting. Thus, I spent my artistic energy on many other works that delighted me and of which I was, and am, proud.

Simply put, I cared far more about art than about the art of war.

I have already mentioned the ill-fated *Last Supper,* and talked also about my favorite one, that some are now calling *Mona Lisa,* and some of the ones I began with Verrocchio, such as *Annunciation*, *The Baptism of Christ*, among others. While in Milan, I painted most of a haunting portrait of *Saint Jerome in the Wilderness*, that reflected how I had felt when Atalante left me. After working for *Il Valentino,* I made a painting of Christ that I love, which showed a beautiful orb, called, of course, *Salvator Mundi.* I painted a luminous *Saint John the Baptist,* for which I used Salaì as its model. It was not easy to get him to sit still long enough for me to paint him. I was most happy with *Lady with an Ermine* and *Saint Anne,* of which I have written extensively.

Who knows if any of these will be known years from now? Am I doomed to obscurity? Well, if that is so, Cecho, at least *you* have loved me, and can keep my memory alive for a time.

LEONARDO'S LETTER

L'Uomo Vetruviano (Vetruvian Man)

When I was living in Milan, my love of mathematics was joined with my love of architecture, as you know, Cecho. I developed a love of studying the ancients, especially Pythagorus, and some friends and I also studied Vetruvius, a Roman architect whom I considered a genius.

Some of us began to wonder, how does one build the perfect church? What are the proper proportions? Vetruvius believed that the dimensions of a house of worship should reflect the proportions of man, as he, it was believed, was built in God's image, and is a shrine to His genius.

Therefore, using myself as a guide, as well as some friends and even cadavers from the morgue, I took over two hundred measurements of the human body, as I wanted to get things just right. Then, I made a circle, with a portrait of myself in the middle, and the protractor jabbed into my navel. I drew a circle showing a perfect arc formed by a man's arms and legs, symbolizing the earth. The square around and above it symbolized the Cosmos, and imbued the entire thing, as a trinity, with the spirit of creation. I was quite proud of my handiwork, especially of the cross-hatched shading of the drawing.

Sadly, this drawing was never used to design a church as far as I could tell, but the men I showed it to were impressed with the work, and I consider it a profound meditation on the mathematical and mystical mystery of humans and our relationship with God, the world, and what lies beyond.

LEONARDO'S LETTER

Matematica

It should be mentioned that one of my great loves is mathematics, the universal language and, along with music, the most beautiful expression of God's patterns in the world. While there in the service of *Il Moro,* I was introduced to a brilliant mathematician, who was also a monk, Fra Luca Pacioli. He had been called to court to lecture from his work, *Summa de Arithmetica,* and the two of us were introduced so that we might solve various engineering problems facing Milan. Around the time I was finishing *The Last Supper,* Luca taught me mathematics, and I learned from him with great gusto. I even illustrated his book, *De Divina Proportione*, where I, of course, got my ideas for *Vetruvian Man*. My friend wanted to develop an overall theory that could unite themes as diverse as the elegant, ancient ideas and formulas of Euclid to useful tasks of modern people. As far as I can tell, he succeeded, and my love of mathematics comes from this time I spent learning from him. Also, need it be said? None of my engineering designs would have been possible had I not learned from this man, the best in his field.

STEVEN FARRINGTON

Breve Intermezzo

The next few years following 1507 I spent going back and forth between Milan and Florence. I did some paintings and murals that I was proud of, such as the last part of *The Battle of Anghiari* for the city hall of Florence, when I had to share space with Michelangelo as he painted a companion piece, the *Battle of Cascina*. As you can imagine, our truce, due to our common enemy, The Prior, was almost completely forgotten as we battled and sniped at each other over the course of those long months when we had to share the same large room. It was horrible having to see that brooding and unpleasant young man every day.

LEONARDO'S LETTER

Leonardo e Michelangelo

So there I was, working across the room from my artistic rival. Michelangelo and I had both been hired to paint things for the city hall, and I had to be across from him every day, as luck would have it.

It was a hot June day, and Michelangelo had stripped to his waist.

Forgive me, dear Cecho, but try as I might to resist, the muscular body of a young man has always been something I can hardly ignore.

We had only exchanged pleasantries up to then, both hoping to keep the peace, when finally, one day, I decided to congratulate him on the success of his *Davide*.

"Grazie, nonno," he said with a wry smile. The lad had taken to treating me as a harmless, if irritating, grandfather, a step up from how he treated me before, if a small one.

"Congratulazioni," I continued, "for making something of value from the legendary Duccio Stone. That was no small feat — even the great Donatello was unable to conquer it," I added.

To this, the young artist merely smirked and replied, "I think we both know I'm better than Donatello," he said.

STEVEN FARRINGTON

The arrogance of that young man! He was lucky he was so handsome, otherwise his cocky attitude would have been truly insufferable.

Finally, one day, I could take it no longer. It had been months since I'd touched a man, and even though I was well past my prime, I still had my natural impulses. I had to steal a look.

I knew it was wrong the way I did it. Michelangelo was lying on his cot in the deserted hall, taking an afternoon nap. I told myself that I was merely studying his nearly perfect, muscular frame as part of my continuing study of human anatomy, useful for my art. After all, wasn't this young man a work of art in his own right?

I drew up beside his cot, and my hungry eyes drank him in like a man who had been wandering in the desert. I studied his face. It was not the handsomest one around, but I admired his square jaw. It was covered with a masculine dark stubble, as Michelangelo had stopped shaving with a penknife, as most young men did in our city.

My eyes gently ran along his delicious body, as I wished my hands could have done. He slept with one hand tucked under his head and a thick mane of dark hair that spilled out over a grimy gray pillow.

My eyes missed nothing of the young man's torso: the tufts of dark hair under his armpit, the exquisite pelt of black hair covering his chiseled, muscular chest, the rippling biceps born of years of labor on unforgiving marble, and, most tantalizing of all, the subtle trail of dark fur that traced an erotic path making its way down the artist's belly, encircling his navel, then disappearing, as if taunting me, into his workman's trousers.

I needed to satisfy my needs, I realized, even if it *was* the unpleasant Michelangelo awakening such lustful feelings in my weak body. However, the sculptor himself stopped me before I could quench the fire of my desire.

His eyes popped open. A brief look of confusion flashed across his face, then recognition, once he realized what was happening.

"Excuse me," I said, backing away. "I was just coming to see if you needed me to clean your brushes," I stammered, noticing the drying implements that lay caked with paint next to his cot and thinking fast.

"Credo di no," he said. "I don't think so, you desperate old troll," he said, his face now covered with a scowl. "You disgust me, Leonardo. Don't ever approach me ever again."

"But I—" I began.

"Never again!" he yelled, starting up and throwing a brush at me.

Paint rained down on my artist's smock as I retreated across the room.

Later that afternoon, as I inspected my paint-splattered face in a mirror in the room I had rented for me and Salaì, I dipped an old cloth in a bowl and slowly wiped the tempera off my thinning, white beard. I studied my weary face with a frown, that countenance with all its cracks and furrows. Had it not been only yesterday that this face had seduced half the men at Verrocchio's bodega? Hadn't my master modeled his David on my beautiful, lithe body and fair visage?

How had it all slipped away? Could time really be that cruel?

*

A few hours later, like a man in a dream, I crept to the edge of the cliff of Mount Ceceri. I briefly wondered how I had come to this place. As if in a trance, I had visited the workshop where I had rented space, rummaged through some old trunks and boxes until I found what I was looking for. Once I had strapped the bat-like wings to my back, I must have been a sight to behold as I walked through Florence, carrying the pulleys and other gear as I headed out of town.

"Master!" a voice called out as I stepped off the edge. It was Salaì, of course, come to find me and watch me fly.

The last thing I thought of before I sailed into the air for what felt like eternity but was probably only a second or two, was how I had yearned for this moment my entire life.

LEONARDO'S LETTER

I plummeted to earth like the falcons and eagles I used to observe as a boy, although far less gracefully. And then, everything went dark.

When I woke up days later, I learned three important facts.

Number one, I had broken several bones, and had almost killed myself in my fall.

Number two, Salaì had almost certainly saved my life by bringing me home and inviting a team of doctors to my bedside to set my bones and care for me until I awoke.

And number three, I learned, to my great and useless sadness, that Mona Lisa Giacondo had died in childbirth.

STEVEN FARRINGTON

Altri Viaggi (Other Travels)

Not much later, I set off again for Milan, heavily in debt and summoned by the French. I expected nothing. I was well over fifty years old, had grown tired, and thought I was finished. How great was my surprise, therefore, when I found myself hailed as a kind of famous genius in that Lombard capital! When I stopped to see my great masterpiece in the dining hall of the monks at *Santa Maria delle Grazie*, I was astounded to find, alongside the brothers preparing for lunch, a flock of young artists studying and trying to reproduce my work on easels. And to think that I had received unending criticism from those same monks just a few years before!

The flaking paint was not as bad as I thought it would be. Perhaps, I thought, the image could survive a few more years. Perhaps I would, as well.

I neglected to mention earlier that my John the Baptist did not recline on Christ's chest, as was the tradition; I reflected on something I had not noticed previously: how much my Jesus seemed alone in this painting. Had I drawn from my own feelings of sadness and regret to show the way he must have felt upon revealing that one of his friends would betray him? As one who has known much sadness and betrayal, I had much from which to draw inspiration.

LEONARDO'S LETTER

Before I knew it, King Louis XII paid me a visit, and hailed me as a great master, something he had not done before. I was suddenly the toast of Milan. I was set up with another property with a vineyard on the edge of the city, and I even had access to a river and the summer retreat of a nobleman, Girolamo, who had been the captain of the Milanese militia. This man, whose surname was Melzi, sent me his adolescent son to take care of me, as this lad had the desire to learn how to paint. Soon, Francesco the student became my full-time valet, disciple, companion, and of course, my lover.

In fact, my dear one, you shortly became the love of my life, something I had given up any hope of finding.

(Now, I am *sure* that my Cecho will hide this memoir well, to avoid the fires of the Inquisition).

Cecho, are you still copying this over, by hand, in a legible left-to-right fashion, so that others may someday read the words of a silly old fool? If you are, then you truly *are* a remarkable man.

My dearest Cecho…I can still remember, as if it were yesterday, the afternoon that you and I became more than friends; you had fashioned a small gondola, stored at your father's villa, in Vaprio d'Adda. We decided to take a short trip that day in the late spring of 1512 to paint landscape views from the river, which I had taken to calling by their French name, *peintures en plein air*. To get us in the mood for painting, we drank a boot of sweet Lombardy wine, and then you decided to strip off your clothes for a swim. I tried to hide my lust for your body. I pretended to look away as you clambered back into our small boat. However, when you complained of being cold, I took you under my cloak to warm you up, like I had with Mirco many years before, and before I knew what was happening, we were caught up in the most passionate embrace of my life. After this, it was an open secret wherever we went that we were lovers. I think that even your father knew the truth. Nevertheless, he was so glad to have his handsome son seen as the disciple to the great Leonardo da Vinci that it seems he pretended to ignore any malicious gossip. After all, I was from Florence, and the idea that a man who prefers the company of men would come from that city was almost to be expected.

Where was I? Oh, yes, I was back in Milan when a combination of Spanish, Swiss, and Venetian forces drove the French from Milan in 1512. I was so used to the French occupiers by that time, I had even begun to perfect my abilities at speaking their language. King Louis had been one of my greatest admirers, and I was sad to see him go. I could never have guessed that I would one day live deep in the French countryside.

I cared little for who ruled Milan, however; I spent most of my time in my villa in Vaprio d'Adda, which is, of course, where I spent my days with you, my dear Cecho!

Soon after this, Leo X assumed the papacy, and, as you know, Cecho, this was the son of Lorenzo di Medici. I could hardly believe my luck; I had met you, my love, and soon we were to head to Rome as guests of the pope!

I had visited the eternal city once before, as the guest of Cesare Borgia, after one of his bloody campaigns, in the autumn of 1502. The Pope, his father, Alexander VI, had only been months away from death when I met him, and he appeared a sick and sad old man, not unlike The Prior, who, despite his crimson robes, velvet cape, and golden skullcap, seemed unhappy and wore a pained expression. I even wondered if he suffered from one of the diseases that sometimes afflict men who bedded too many women.

During that trip, I visited Hadrian's Villa at Tivoli and got some ideas for sculpting, painting, and developed a greater appreciation for ancient Roman architecture.

After the Borgia pope died in 1503, there had been Pope Julius, who was considered a decent enough pontiff. And now, Leo X.

When I returned in 1513, as an invitee of Leo X, I was treated as a special guest, at least at first. The Medici no longer saw me as a simple pawn in their game of chess as Lorenzo had done so many years before. Now, I was a force to be reckoned with, an accomplished and successful artist.

Dear Cecho, you were often with me then, although you did spend some of that time with your family back in Milan. I will summarize this time quickly for posterity. I have come this far, so I may as well try to finish this foolish account of my life.

Despite my successes, I had missed out on my chance to decorate the Sistine Chapel, and to do anything meaningful for the Vatican. Years before, when I was sent to Milan in the 1480s, various friends and colleagues had had that pleasure, such as Botticelli, Perugino, and later, even Rafael. And then, of course, my old rival Michelangelo was invited to paint the ceiling of the chapel, which infuriated me to no end. I must say that I went to Rome with high hopes, but these were to be dashed.

Although I was put up in the Belvedere Courtyard and the Apostolic Palace, and given an allowance of thirty-three ducats per month, I was given only minor jobs while in Rome. The new pontiff *did* seem to want me to paint something, as he had seen sketches of my work, but I soon found myself ignored and sidelined. I cannot prove it, of course, but I suspect The Prior, whom I think may have had Leo's ear, of undermining my career. Of course, I cannot deny that I still had the reputation of a man who did not finish what he started, despite my brilliance.

I swear that, after a few months, I began to see the old Prior, my enemy, lurking around the Papal Palace. Was he truly there, or was I merely imagining him? If it *was* him, what was he doing there? Was he spying on me? Did he intend to ruin me, have me punished, or worse? How was he still alive, at that advanced age? I never told you, my dear, about those fears and nightmares I had of The Prior. Rather, I tried my best to keep busy, hoping to take my mind off him.

I worked on plans to drain various marshes surrounding Rome, the Pontine Marshes, and continued to dissect cadavers. I tried to have the pope publish my findings, but he demurred. I spent time in the Vatican City Gardens practicing botany, and taking notes, developed a new kind of varnish, as the experience of the flaking of the paint from *The Last Supper* haunted me. Perhaps, I thought, if I created the perfect clear covering, any painting, such as my great Milanese masterpiece, could be protected from the scourge of time. Sadly, this dream, like so many others, was to elude me.

Oh, yes. Now would be a good time for me to write more about *The Last Supper*.

STEVEN FARRINGTON

L'Ultima Cena, The Last Supper

I realize now that I never finished writing about my time painting *The Last Supper*, which was shortly after I adopted Salaì.

I spent over three years on that masterpiece, which was a perfect marriage, if I may say so, of emotion, artistic excellence, and mathematical perspective. Simply put, this work unites our earthly world with the divine. However, as much as I put my whole heart into this work, that very part of me was to be broken by this project.

While working on *Il Cenacolo,* as we always called it, I wanted to do two things: I wanted to honor traditions associated with this important moment, when Christ reveals his greatest betrayal, but I also wanted to *innovate*. I would make this fresco something different, something revolutionary. My own special creation.

As Verrocchio always told me: "Learn and pay homage to those who came before you, Leonardo; then, once you have done so, break the rules you have mastered. Go beyond, transcend the tradition. Make the work your own. Listen to that spirit of creativity that lives inside every artist."

LEONARDO'S LETTER

I knew that, if I failed to bring out that part of my spirit which I held inside of me, not doing so would destroy me.

In any case. Duke Ludovico, *Il Moro,* had called me into his study one day in 1494. "We're making some public works on and inside various churches in the city," he said. Ludovico was convinced of the importance of making his imprint felt on the Lombard capital, anything to justify his grip on the duchy.

"One of these will be *Santa Maria delle Grazie,*" he said. I remembered walking past that house of God and feeling a tug of something like a premonition months before. "It's a church with a monastery attached," the duke continued, "and they're renovating and expanding the refectory. This is where you will put a fresco depicting the last time Christ dined with his men, and the first Eucharist," he said. "Make something nice for the brothers to look at when they break bread," he said, dismissing me with a wave.

And so, that is what I did.

I threw myself into the task. I spent months planning what I would do to make this my *capolavoro,* my greatest masterpiece. Luckily, Ludovico let me do the work on my own schedule, and he passed the planning of pageants and plays to other, newer courtiers who were lower in the pecking order than I.

STEVEN FARRINGTON

I made a great many calculations when planning this fresco. But beyond the mathematical excellence and colors of the composition, I wished to show the human side of both Christ and his apostles. They had been saints and the Son of God, yes, but I also yearned to show them as *people*. Instead of adding halos, as had always been done, I decided to show each man in his own imperfect, unadorned humanity. I would put my knowledge of the human body and emotions to maximal use. I would capture the chaos of the moment after Christ revealed the terrible truth about the betrayal, yet I also wanted beauty and order coupled *with* that chaos. Christ would be the calm at the center of the storm, a picture of absolute equanimity and sagacity. Indeed, *my* Jesus would not only be the son of God, but also a tranquil man of wisdom, accepting, even *celebrating* the fate that he had chosen, reaching for the bread and wine to begin the institution of the holy rite that Christians would adhere to forever after.

In another famous work, I painted a baby Jesus wrestling with a lamb, the very symbol of the passion which he must have struggled with. By painting him the way I did here, I showed him accepting his fate and coming to terms with that struggle.

Instead of placing Judas on the opposite side of the table, I would depict him on the same side as the others, since his betrayal, shown by the pouch of silver pieces, was all part of the divine plan. Like Jesus, Judas would reach for a bowl, the same one symbolizing the role that both he and Jesus had agreed upon. Jesus could have passed the cup to another, but instead had embraced his fate and sacrificed his life for humanity. And he could not have done so without Judas.

This way, I wanted to show to the viewer that whatever happens, even sins can be part of a divine plan.

Did I embed a special code into this fresco? Why certainly. I am a mathematician, am I not?

As everyone knows, the number twelve is mystical. However, I arranged my disciples and Christ in such a way that it would be a special code for my fellow sinners and outcasts, something men like me knew that resonated in our bones. We sinners of the "fine eye" had whispered this passage to each other for years, the one that said that no one is cast off from the Lord forever. The message of universal salvation and God's unequivocal love for all is to be found in Lamentations 3, verses 31 to 33. Therefore, I arranged the men in the 3-3-1-3-3 formation, with Christ in the center.

But apart from this mathematical message that only a few would understand, I hoped to create something visually moving. Part of what I was trying to achieve with this work, to put it simply, was something that drew the viewer in. The walls and the ceiling in the piece led the viewer's eye to Christ in the center of the fresco, and indeed, I planned the vanishing point on Jesus's forehead. The eye is drawn right to Christ, as he is the center of the life for Christians and for His Church.

How ironic that I, an eccentric hedonistic humanist, would create such a work, but I can contain multitudes of contrasting and conflicting parts of my character.

God is love, and Christ is his messenger. This is what I believed, and still do, at least in my nobler moments. And no one is so far gone so that divine love will be denied forever. Even Dante told us that Inferno, limbo, and separation from divine love is only temporary. And Jesus, both divine and completely human, was sent, in my opinion, to personify God's love. And this message is the center of the life of any Christian.

Perhaps, I thought, if my old enemy The Prior had seen a painting like this, one that put a loving and kind Jesus front and center for him to study every day, a human Christ who loved people unconditionally, knowing that *no one* was a lost cause, perhaps he would have turned out differently. Perhaps, through my work, I could help to create a Church culture of priests and monks dedicated to loving and serving *all* people, instead of judging them. Perhaps the men of the cloth would act as loving shepherds gently guiding lost sheep home, instead of trying to kill the sheep who had gone off exploring.

I began to see this as a holy mission, my reason for getting up every morning…what the French love to call their *"raison d'être." This* was why I had been put on the earth, I decided. Not only was I a talented man who could paint and create beautiful pieces of art, I began to see myself as a prophet, not unlike Elijah or Moses, heroes who left their people and returned with a magical message of hope, the elixir they needed, but failed to realize how much.

I threw myself into this project for over three years. I even moved into the convent, assisted not only by Salaì, but also by Giampietrino, Andrea Solari, and Cesare de Sesto. I would often work from sundown to sunset on the project, standing on the paint-stained scaffolding taking measurements, sometimes forgetting to eat or drink for an entire day, and often working late into the night. The brothers of the convent laughed heartily one morning when they found a basin full of my urine that Salaì had collected, loath as I was to break the spell of my work even for a few minutes. Yet, they also scratched their heads in puzzlement when I often failed to appear for several days. This was time I spent tormented in my room, making measurements or sketches of each saint, fighting with myself to get each gesture, every look, perfect, or as close to perfect as possible, sleeping only a few hours at a stretch before taking up the pen or the quill or the brush again and again.

I should address something I have heard whispered over the years, often in relation to *The Last Supper*. Some have wondered if I was a Mason, and I have never denied this rumor, as it saved my life once when The Prior accused me of attending the same mysterious gatherings that he did. It was easier to imply being a spiritual descendent of the Templars than the alternative. However, it must be said that I was not trying to send any specific message about Jesus and Mary Magdalene with this work. Perhaps Saint John the Baptist looks feminine here, not unlike my mother, and I may have left this ambiguous for the viewer to interpret, but I was not attempting to send a secret message about Our Lady.

My message, as I have said, was one of God's universal love for all, and of Jesus's — and his apostles' — humanity.

I was so proud and astonished when, finally, I looked up at my work in February 1498 and realized it was done. When some of the monks came in to see the final work, several of them fell to their knees. It was then that I realized that I had succeeded in creating something of beauty and transcendent meaning, a work that would belong to the ages. Just like Mother Mary, I had been pierced by Logos, and had survived. And this was my holy child, my babe, no less than if I had given birth to it in a stable.

You can imagine my sense of devastation when, the following year, I returned to revisit my treasured masterpiece to find the paint flaking off the rectory wall. Jesus' feet had even been cut away to build a door. A *door*, Cecho! Can you imagine? The sacrilege of those Philistines!

The paint of Judas's cloak was already coming off in bits. I rushed to the wall. Beads of moisture were sitting right on the cloak! My eyes flew to James the Major, who, through my vanity, I had made as a self-portrait, and I was horrified to see some of the tip of my own nose missing!

LEONARDO'S LETTER

Was I being punished by God for my vanity? This had been painted in 1497, after all, when the bonfire of the same name had burned in Florence...

Would a doubting Thomas no longer point to heaven in a few years' time? Would his flaking finger be unable to check Christ's wound after the Resurrection? Would Saint Paul be unable to lunge forward with a knife in a vain but valiant attempt to save Our Lord? Would my entire creation be lost?

Perhaps *this* was what I got, I thought ruefully, for experimenting with oil paints *and* tempera. When I had been painting, the plaster had been dry, but now, it seemed, the whole environment of the room had changed. Or, worse yet, had I been wrong about the plaster all along, too blind to see what was right in front of my eyes?

"What is *in* this structure?" I demanded to know, grabbing one of the workmen and shoving him against the wall.

"Master Leonardo," the man said, trembling, "we thought you knew. We filled these walls with rubble. We only thought this wall would be temporary."

"Why would it be only *temporary*?" I almost yelled. "By building it that way, moisture will be trapped in, and on, the wall so easily. Didn't you see what I went through, just to make this fresco stand the test of time?"

"We thought the painting was only supposed to be for a short while, something nice and decorative," the builder said, scratching his head. "You could always paint it again."

"I can't," I said, my voice full of exasperation. I sank down on the clay floor of the dining room. "Cesare Borgia is closing in, and this is where he will find me shortly. There's no time to redo it."

"Well," the man said, stepping back and studying the wall. "It still looks good enough to me," he said. "I bet it could last a good ten or twenty years, easily."

Tears streamed down my face, and then I began to laugh.

"You know what the monks say," the man said, trying to cheer me up. *"Sic transit gloria mundi."*

"Of course," I said. "I didn't expect it to last *forever,* but more than a few years would have been nice."

"Well, that's how it goes," the man said with a chuckle.

"Why do I even bother?" I asked no one in particular. "I may as well just hire myself out to Borgia to help him devise instruments of war."

"That sounds like a good plan," the man said, obviously blissfully unaware of the anguish that consumed me. "You'd probably make a lot more money that way," he said helpfully.

STEVEN FARRINGTON

Bologna

Back, once again, and for a final time, to politics — of the papal, and the earthly, variety.

I was, as you may remember, quite bored during my time in Rome. I had toyed with the idea of writing my memoirs then, and perhaps I should have done so. In any case, I was cast aside, for reasons that are still unclear to me, in the papal court. My work was not valued. I fell ill, and thank God, Cecho, you were there to care for me. It was then that my body began to fail me, although I was able to hide it well.

I felt tormented during that time. I was ill and alone. My masterpiece was dying slowly in Milan. My career was over. Had it all been for nothing?

I still would swear that I caught occasional glimpses of The Prior as he stole through the shadows of the Vatican. I imagined that he had come to torment and try to destroy me. I could not be sure that my failing health had not made me delirious, but still he haunted my dreams and some of my waking moments when I felt full of dread.

He, and a disastrous flood, brought on by my pride, sent to punish me. Or worse yet, the flames of the Inquisition, or those of an angry God, like those sent down on Sodom and Gomorrah.

LEONARDO'S LETTER

The weed, I feared, had been finally separated from the wheat, and was just waiting to be consumed by the furnace, where there would be the gnashing of teeth and great howls of suffering.

Soon, news came down to us in Rome that the French were invading again, and this time, they had recaptured Milan and were heading further south at lightning speed. Leading their forces was a new and dynamic king, known as François the First.

The pope threw a fit of rage, angry, of course, at having the French invading his backyard, and wanting the entire collection of Italian city states for the Medici, now that the Borgias seemed finally to be all vanquished or dead.

"Pack your bags, Leonardo, and prepare your servants," he spat at me when I was summoned to the papal apartments. "You're going with me to Bologna. I don't speak French, and I need you as an interpreter. We need to parlay with them."

You, my dear Cecho, were back at home, safe in Milan, and unable to support your Leonardo in his hour of need.

Little did I suspect the trap awaiting me.

STEVEN FARRINGTON

La Battaglia Finale

Two days later, I stood next to the pope and across from the new King of France outside a lecture hall at the ancient University of Bologna. One of the last official things I would do was to interpret for these two men, for my French had grown strong in Milan as I had worked with French painters to try, in vain, to save my flaking masterpiece.

"I am the new Duke of Milan," King François said. "And now, my men have also occupied Bologna."

"But surely, you shall come no further," the pontiff said, and the many prelates and officials gasped at this implication, as he seemed willing to allow the French to remain in Italian lands. He appeared not to want to insist that they withdraw. Would they remain there, occupying the whole north of Italy?

"That remains to be seen," the French king replied.

"I protest!" came a voice from behind me, and I froze. I knew that voice. It belonged to a man who had been haunting me for forty years.

"This is an abomination!" The Prior said, stepping forward out of the shadows. "How dare you let the words of His Holiness be translated by a man such as *this*," cried my old enemy, pointing at me, accusing me with a bony old index finger.

"What do you mean by these words?" asked the French king, looking both cross and surprised at the insolence of the interruption.

"This *man*," he said, glancing at me with disdain, "this…this heretic, this human scum you see before you, is not fit to be in the company of kings *nor* popes," he said.

I looked to the pope, who glanced away from me. Had he planned this, or at least allowed my old enemy to ambush me in this way? In exchange for what?

The French king looked annoyed, and soon this annoyance seemed to grow to anger.

"Is this not the great Leonardo da Vinci?" he asked, his voice booming and filling the room. "Is this not the great man, the superb engineer and artist?"

At this, the pope looked confused, and The Prior simply scoffed. "The great *finocchio*," he sneered, and I translated this for the French king as an artist with a fine eye. I think I used the words *"fin oeil."*

François seemed to consider this for a long moment.

I held my breath. I found myself staring at a spiral and then a plinth of one of the pillars holding up this great hall.

"What, exactly, are you accusing him of?" the king asked.

"I'm glad you asked!" The Prior said, his voice rising. "He will finally burn for his sins, sins that I can prove, with various witnesses." He pointed his bony finger at me again, his dark eyes burning like a lake in Hell. "I accuse this man of *sodomy!*" he cried, and there was an audible gasp from the assembled multitude.

"Sodomia!" he cried.

There was no need to translate this word into French.

I felt my heart fall to my feet. Was this it? Would I die in the painful fires of the Inquisition? Was this the horrendous end of Leonardo? Instead of a flood, was I, in fact, to be consumed by fire?

The king stared straight ahead, and I saw something play over his face that was hard to read.

"Guards," he finally said, and a group of French guards came forward.

"Throw that man in the dungeon right now," he said. And when the guards came toward me, the king said, "No, not *him*. Throw that disgusting old slanderer in the deepest place you can find, and then have him beheaded first thing tomorrow morning."

There was another gasp from the crowd as I translated into Italian what had been commanded.

The pope started to protest, but the king cut him off.

"I have seen Leonardo's great work, *The Last Supper*, in Milan," he said. "That work was clearly the work of a great master, a man of divine power and inspiration," he said. "I have ordered my best men to do whatever needs to be done to preserve it."

The pope began, once again to protest, but the French king turned to leave, then stopped, half turning to the papal party to add, "We will remain in Milan. And Leonardo is coming with *me*. Clearly, Italy doesn't deserve him."

STEVEN FARRINGTON

Amboise

So, my dear Cecho, you know the rest. Soon, we were brought here by my great friend François. I have been happy here in Amboise, these last two years.

I never bothered to find out what happened to The Prior, but I assume that his head was removed from his body as François had ordered. In any case, I endeavor not to feel any joy in imagining this, try as I do to love everyone. But, of course, in my least noble moments, I feel a small spark of joy in knowing what likely happened to him, which I do at least *try* to suppress.

One day, on one of our walks through the countryside along the Loire River, I asked François why he had saved me. He could just as easily have let me die.

To this, he just smiled at me, and said that he saw what I had done with my composition of *The Last Supper*.

"How so?" I asked, and the king simply replied, *"Trois, trois, un, trois, trois,"* and this was all I needed to know.

*

My dear one, this is, perhaps, enough for now. If I feel like writing more tomorrow, or the next day, I may revisit this project. Or perhaps not. My eyes and hand grow weary. I hope that you will hide these scandalous writings well, whatever the case.

Before I go, however, let me share one final thought; as loath as I am to admit it, I must confess something equally as unforeseen as my falling in true love at such an advanced age.

I must admit that, even though part of me feels sad and isolated in this faraway Château of the Clos Lucé, as the guest of the French king, I have noticed myself once again having strange thoughts regarding God and of man's place in Creation.

Even though I have spent my life studying the world with logic, questioning everything, studying all the ways of nature, the swirls, twirls, and spirals of it all, the mathematical laws of the ages, I feel my spirit longing for something more.

Perhaps I have spent too much time painting works of spiritual importance. Maybe I spent too much time, as well, hiding away from my great enemy in a friendly church. Perhaps, despite myself, I have become something I could never have foreseen:

A fervent believer.

Just like the song goes, *"Sicut Cervus desiderat ad fonts aquarum, ita desiderat anima mea ad te, Deus."*

My heart, like a stag seeking water, yearns for God's love.

STEVEN FARRINGTON

Like the birds I used to set free, I feel my soul rising heavenward every night when I close my eyes.

My mind is in a fight with itself. Part of me yearns for logic and proof, yet another part longs for the irrational, a connection with the divine.

I dare say that I am coming around again to something of a full circle, back to the child I once was, the one who peered into that fearsome cave so long ago.

Now, of course, I do not peer into a hole in the ground but rather into a new one, the gaping knowledge of my impending mortality.

What will it all have meant?

Perhaps something of what I have created or discovered can help my fellow creatures after all. One can hope. I want to leave the world with more joy and love than death and sadness, better than how I found it.

I certainly hope that the beauty and art I leave behind can atone for the instruments of war that I designed. Please, God, I pray that it be so.

As a well-spent day brings happy sleep, so a life well spent brings happy death. My life has been well spent, and now I am ready to meet a happy death, whenever it comes for me.

These days, as I wander along the river, you, my darling Cecho at my side supporting me and holding my

LEONARDO'S LETTER

arm, I feel something tugging at my spirit. Perhaps it is simply the knowledge of love, or old age, or the gentle feeling of being at the end of a life well lived…but, from time to time, on certain days, I feel the hint of a suggestion that perhaps there is an underlying spirit that connects us all to one another. Call it God, call it love, call it what you will. It is not unlike how I felt when Father Giuseppe sang his mass in Santa Maria Novella, (*Agnus Dei* three times through), or how I felt when I finished a great work of art and stepped back to admire what I had helped bring forth.

It is a thing I cannot explain, a subject I cannot draw, much less paint. But this feeling I have of connection…it allows me not to fear entering this final cave, the cave of death.

I have known great love, my spirit has flown, and my life has had meaning. Thanks to all of this, I know, now, as in my youth, that what I will find beyond will be something divine, something marvelous and something extraordinary.

Something that's part of an adventure.

My life is, indeed, ending in a great flood. It is a flood of feeling, a flood of beauty, of peace, and, most of all, a flood of love.

My cup runneth over with love.

The End

Made in the USA
Monee, IL
02 October 2023